Looking
for Work

SUSAN
CHEEVER

SIMON AND SCHUSTER NEW YORK

For C. T.

Pickwick goes through life with that godlike gullibility which is the key to all adventures. The greenhorn is the ultimate victor in everything; it is he that gets the most out of life. . . . His soul will never starve for exploits or excitements who is wise enough to be made a fool of. He will make himself happy in the traps that have been laid for him; he will roll in their nets and sleep. All doors will fly open to him who has a mildness more defiant than mere courage. The whole is unerringly expressed in one fortunate phrase— he will be always "taken in." To be taken in everywhere is to see the inside of everything. It is the hospitality of circumstance. With torches and trumpets, like a guest, the greenhorn is taken in by Life. And the skeptic is cast out by it.

—FROM G. K. Chesterton's
Charles Dickens, the Last of the Great Men

chapter 1

For as long as I can remember my father has been the Regius Professor of Comparative Literature at Columbia, and his connection with the University goes back even further than that. In fact, my mother was one of his students, Barbara Palmer from Buffalo, New York. She was the second daughter of a rich and socially comfortable family, who had been caught up by the social changes of the 1930s and was just enough of a rebel to insist on going to college in New York City instead of to Wheaton or Smith. And just rebel enough to stay married to a college professor.

Of course, my father wasn't your ordinary Columbia professor. He had the mind and manners of an intellectual Bostonian, and it was sheer perversity as far as I could ever figure out that kept him from moving north to teach at Harvard. Especially when, after his book on the novelist André Gide, *Literary Cubism*, won the National Book Award, President Pusey offered him the prestigious Swansdown

Chair in French Literature. Who knows. Sometimes I think he was a little afraid that at Harvard there would be other men like him—that he would be less special. He certainly stood out on the Columbia campus with his flinty blue eyes and carefully parted white hair and his blackthorn stick. The only East Sider at a West Side university, the only devout Episcopalian attending services at the Rose and Murray Schwartz Memorial Chapel for Ecumenical Worship, the only broad *a* in the Bronx, and certainly the only Columbia Professor who still occasionally rode with the Myopia Hunt.

So I had French and piano and ballet lessons and elaborate birthday parties at our Sutton Place apartment in the winter, and sailing on Nantucket Sound or riding at our place in Connecticut in the summer, just like other post-Victorian pre-teens. But in many ways my life was very different from the lives of my friends at the Lycée on East Seventy-second Street or at the barre in Madame Natasha's classes. My parents' friends were writers and professors and scholars, and although a few of them shared my parents' liberal ambivalence—shuttling with some difficulty between proper society and the world of the intellectual elite—many of them did not. Our spacious living room with its grand views of the East River was often crowded with a kind of man my maternal grandparents would have heartily detested. Shabby academics in worn-out tweeds, men who chain smoked Camels or Chesterfields, drank their whiskey neat, and spent hours arguing the relative merits of I. A. Richards or Christopher Isherwood. I once saw an old friend of my father's who was visiting us from Oxford (he was the master of Balliol College at the time) leave the room with a thrilling string of curses because someone had insisted on rating Dr. Leavis above Tom Eliot.

Naturally, my father's friends fascinated me, made my lessons and recitals and my mother's prim tea-time ladies seem boring, and so I joined these academic conclaves long before I understood what they were all about.

"Oh, good, here comes Salley," Ralph Ellison or old Dr. Biddle or Robert Penn Warren would say as I hurried through the living room door in the late afternoon after school. "I know she'll be on my side."

Well, with that kind of background you might suppose I would have the sense to think twice about marrying into another academic family, or about falling in love with the son of a colleague and old friend of my father's, or even about getting involved with an editor or a writer at all. But of course, that's exactly what happened.

Not that I was so sure.

At the time, I was a just-out-of-Radcliffe reporter on the *Laramie* (Wyoming) *Eagle* (circulation nine thousand), the only newspaper that offered me a job when I graduated from college with a gentlewoman's C— average. When Jason called me from New York to propose, at first I said no. He would have to wait, I said. But it was a bad week at work, nothing on the police blotter but fender-benders and public intoxication arrests, a tedious Board of Selectmen's meeting to cover, and a nasty letter to the editor from the Superintendent of Schools about a story I had written. Driving back in the twilight Friday night to the ramshackle little house I had rented on Charley Bailey's sheep ranch, I was assailed by a wave of uncertainty and loneliness. The snow on the mountains turned red in the setting sun. My life there and my professional ambitions seemed empty and silly. I called Jason and agreed to come back to New York and live with him for a while and we would see.

"I love you, Salley," he said.

So I flew in from sheep ranching and the ski slopes, the grimy clatter of the *Eagle* city room, and driving home at night through falling snow, and landed with a thump in Jason Gardens' dark bedroom on an airshaft at the back of a brownstone on Perry Street.

The first few days and weeks glided by in a soft blur. In the morning, through the mists of sleep I would hear Jason carefully making fresh coffee for himself before he left for his office at *American Magazine*. When the door clicked shut behind him and I heard him double lock it from the outside, I drifted back into the comforting darkness and slept until early afternoon. Then I would get up, go out and do the shopping at Balducci's and Comollo's Meat Market and the other village stores where Jason had charge accounts. At about five o'clock I would take a long shower, fix two drinks, and start waiting for him to come home. We were very much in love, everybody said so.

On Saturday mornings Jason put on his old blue jeans and a polo shirt and went whistling off to cooking class at James Beard's house. I took the F train uptown to visit my parents. I guess they were pleased that I was with Jason; they were old friends of his parents and Jason's father had taught for a while at Columbia before *he* went north to Yale. But I could tell they were nervous because I never said anything about getting married. We sat in the living room and made polite literary conversation. We shared a light lunch prepared by Florence. Nothing was said. Let's not pressure her. On Saturday afternoons Jason would come home and cook for the two of us, trying out what he had learned in the morning. The properties of cream, the liaison of flour and butter, the miracle of béchamel. And after dinner and wine and thick strong coffee in tiny white cups we took each other to bed.

Once we went to a party at the Soviet Mission on East Sixty-seventh Street for the poet Yevtushenko. Leonard Bernstein was there and the Arthur Millers and my parents and there were lobster and ice cream set out on plywood tables covered with green cloth in what looked like a high school classroom.

"But I had no idea you would be so beautiful," said Yevtushenko when we shook hands, pulling me toward him for a Russian bearhug.

He exaggerated. But I was a pretty girl, with shoulder-length light brown hair, dark eyes and regular features. Medium height with a curvy body and full breasts, I would examine myself in the mirror in Jason's bathroom with a mixture of pleasure and dread. Plump but firm and athletic, my body glowed in the dim fluorescent light. I could look awful or wonderful—clean hair, a good mood and the right clothes made all the difference. And that night in a black dress I had hurriedly bought at Bonwit's and the big gold loop earrings we all wore in the Sixties, I looked pretty good.

"You look very grown-up," my mother said as I kissed her goodnight. (A touch of silk, a whiff of perfume.)

But I wasn't at all.

At first, instead of going to a psychiatrist I turned to people I knew. I called a boyfriend of my college roommate, Annie; he had a Master's Degree in behavioral psychology and lived in a one-room apartment in Brooklyn Heights with a view of the Manhattan skyline. He was reading the *Bhagavad Gita* and he had put a mattress in the bathroom for meditating. That was all. The Manhattan skyline, as he patiently explained, was his furniture. So we sat on the wooden floor, backs propped up against the dusty walls, and drank weak tea and talked about his prospects of getting a good teaching job at Berkeley. Annie was in graduate school there.

"I know you now," he called after me as I clattered down five flights of wooden stairs on my way out. "I know you will do the right thing if you listen to your own heart."

Very helpful.

Then I went to a real psychiatrist with black leather couches and track lighting in his office and a gold watch nestled in the coarse dark hair on his wrist.

"So you're not sure if you want to get married?" he said, leaning back in his chair and pressing his fingertips together. "Well, I wouldn't worry about it if I were you, dear. Most young ladies your age would give their eyeteeth to be in your position." Sixty dollars, please.

There was no reason not to get married. I was a lucky girl to have Jason; a lot of people have no one. I loved his cooking. But the decision eluded me, and in the end I had to trick my wary self into that final joining.

It was a warm afternoon at the end of March, the spring sun was melting the last of the street snow and water dripped off the window sills; I had already done the shopping and taken my shower. Jason was at work, and I was bored. I didn't know then that indecision is in itself a decision. And so, with nothing better to do on that warm afternoon I thought I would just stroll uptown and look at wedding dresses. Just *look* at them, just in *case*. I took the F train up to Forty-second Street and walked down past the Public Library to Lord & Taylor in the balmy air. It was a beautiful day and people were smiling and walking with their coats thrown over their arms. But the minute I arrived at the Bride's Department on the store's second floor, the mood vanished. I immediately felt out of place. The room seemed crowded with the kind of long-limbed blond girl that had been very, very popular at Miss Singer's School. Two of them were dressed up like lacy white confections with salesladies and bridesmaids-to-be oohing and aahing over them. Their mothers looked on approvingly from white satin sofas. Shoppers passing by in the corridor got a glimpse of these young butterflies in the gold-framed full-length mirror and smiled to each other. This is the happiest day of your life.

On me, nothing fit. Hadn't I even set a date? No, there were no dresses that could be made in time for an early May wedding. Why was I in such a rush? (Was I pregnant or something? And in that case, young lady, the Bride's Department of Lord & Taylor is no place for you!) Where was my mother, anyway? At Saks and Bonwit's and Bendel's it was the same story. Perhaps a sample dress could be altered for me in time, but hadn't I ordered the invitations yet? Didn't I also need wedding pictures and bridesmaids' dresses? Only mothers know these essential things.

The search for a dress took on a lonely momentum of its own. In the beginning, I didn't even want to get married. But soon, all I cared about was being one of those white and gleaming lighthearted butterfly brides-to-be. Smiled on by the whole world. At peace with society. In tune with nature and respected by salesladies.

I called my mother on the telephone.

"I'm shopping for a wedding dress," I told her. "I wonder if you would like to come and help me?"

"Congratulations, dear," she said.

chapter 2

And so the fete commenced. There were letters to be written telling the happy news, and relatives to be summoned from faraway places for the great ceremony. There were wedding photographs to be taken, and newspaper announcements to be composed, and the guest list and the bridesmaids' dresses and the ushers' gifts and the music and the flowers and the limousine and the cake. Jason and I spent Thursday evenings with Father Harry Bingham going over the Episcopal instructions to a couple about to be married.

Dearly beloved, we are gathered together here in the sight of God . . .

The day we went to pick up the engraved invitations at Cartier was the day of the Vietnam Moratorium March down Fifth Avenue. There were traffic jams everywhere, some of the side streets were blocked off by riot troops in flak jackets and green helmets, and there were police sharpshooters on the roofs of Fifth Avenue and the Hotel Pierre. We, however, were on our way to Connecticut to spend the weekend addressing wedding invitations. Black ink. First the outer envelope with the name and address from the master list, then the inner envelope with the name. Write, open, write, turn over. *Dr. and Mrs. Charles Potter request* . . . Jason and I double parked the car and ran hand in hand through the ornate portico of Cartier to get the creamy, heavy vellum-wrapped packages.

On Fifth Avenue, our countrymen, our colleagues, our good friends and lovers-to-be marched with a grim and conscientious step. Past the Plaza Hotel where we had booked a room for the wedding night. Past Bonwit's where we finally got the bridesmaids' dresses. Past Tiffany where we bought the rings. Past Cartier. What on earth were we doing there? Standing gawking on the sidewalk like creatures from another planet. Were we marching to a different drummer?

Or were we just out of it?

The dress was beautiful, a gleaming cocoon of soft white silk and creamy lace that made me glow. It hung, sweetly innocent, in its Henri Bendel plastic dress bag in Jason's tiny closet on Perry Street during the days before the wedding. I often wished I was in there with it.

There was a dinner party at the Blacks'. Gerry Black worked with Jason on the magazine and their colleagues mixed indifferently with my few friends. My maid of honor, a roommate from my sophomore year, was kosher and couldn't eat the elaborate lobster Newburg that Barbara Black had spent a week preparing. There was a prenuptial dinner at Lüchow's restaurant with sweet May wine, veal baked in greasy breadcrumbs and an Oom Pah Pah band of middle-aged men in lederhosen that drowned out conversations. Not that there was much to say. I felt anxious and left out. Over the din, my parents complained about the food and the bill.

There were other disasters too, disasters that drew sweet Jason and me together in bonds of resistance instead of bonds of matrimony. Four days before the wedding, his mother had a mild heart attack. His father was on the phone, asking him to drive up to their house in Connecticut to see her; Jason looked pale, his skin flattened against the bones of his face.

"I just don't think I can get out there, Pop," he said. "Let me speak to Mother."

"The only men who ever wear wedding rings," she took this opportunity to inform him from her sickbed, "are traveling salesmen who are trying to cheat on their wives."

("You know, I'd like to wear a ring too," Jason had said. It seemed like years ago.)

The last night before the ceremony we all sat around the hotel room where some of the guests were staying and talked. And I guess we learned the hard way what we should have known all along. A wedding isn't for the bride and groom, it's for their family and friends. The B. and G. are just props, silly stick figures with no more significance than the pink and white candy figures on the top of the cake. I didn't know that then, though, and I cried all night. Poor Jason, confused and maybe miserable too, trying to comfort me with caresses in our dreary bedroom. I wept, oh how I wept, for my own loneliness and for the loneliness of the whole world, for the loneliness of the about-to-be-married and the loneliness of the separated and divorced. For little children lost in foreign airports and pets abandoned on the beach at the end of the summer, and old people in tenements looking out their windows at the city streets on hot days. At last at dawn we fell asleep, lost children too, curled against each other for warmth.

The wedding of Jason and Salley was a great success. It later became a famous literary party that people talked about at other famous literary parties. The church grounds had been covered with Astro Turf and a yellow-and-white-striped tent. Philip Roth was there, and John Cheever, and my Aunt Janie from Grosse Pointe, Michigan.

"I hope you'll call me," Phil said, "I have someone who cooks dinner now."

The bride was drunk on champagne. The dress wrinkled. It was raining and the limousine got lost in the twisting side streets on the way to the church. The best man almost forgot to hand over the ring—he was trying to pick out the literary celebrities in the first two pews.

Into this holy estate these two persons present come now to be joined. If any man can show just cause . . .

At the reception, Jason's two little girls from his first marriage were hysterical, and there was no one to take care of them. The *Book for Brides* that we studied hadn't said anything about stepchildren. They panicked. At ages six and eight they were unable to join in the literary banter. They didn't know about the Russian dissidents, or Andrei Vosnesensky's visit to the United States, or Saul Bellow's latest novel, *Herzog.* They thought they were losing their father. They wouldn't leave his side. Charlotte clung, weeping, to the tails of Jason's frock coat.

"Pick me up, Daddy," she cried. "Please pick me up."

To placate them, to keep them from spoiling the swell party with their sobs and tears, we—the so-called grownups—turned the wedding over to them—the so-called children. They cut the cake, they headed the reception line, they had portraits taken by the photographer in their delicate pink dresses. Rice and rose petals were thrown at them.

And when we ran out to the car at the end of the party,

laughing and together at last, there they were in the back
seat.

*Forasmuch as Jason and Salley have consented together
in holy wedlock, and have witnessed the same before God
and this company, and thereto have given and pledged their
troth . . . I pronounce that they are man and wife.*

The past was already upon us. We did get away finally,
but we were already working on our private lists of angers
and disappointments. Jason was in agonies of guilt. He had
been forced to rebuff his children and to fail his ailing
mother. I didn't understand guilt, then, but I felt right away
that some terrible mistake had been made. Lying on our
wedding-night bed at the Plaza, I pretended to be asleep
and thought about old boyfriends: Harry, and Mike
Abrams, and Annie's brother David. I should have married
Mike, I thought, I should have married Mike. Later we went
to dinner downstairs in the gloomy vaults of the Oak Room.
The elevator mirrors showed me a plump child-woman in a
cotton piqué dress and patent-leather party shoes.

We spent a week in New Hampshire at my Grandmother
Palmer's house where I had spent happy and confusing
childhood summers. Jason had never been there and he
hated it. It was out-of-season-cold-and-rainy, and on the first
morning we were there the telephone on the bedside table
woke us up at eight o'clock.

"How *was* it, dear?" my Grandmother Palmer wanted to
know.

It was awful, but my lips were sealed by the wedding ceremony. My complaints would have to be private now. What
a humiliation, what a disgrace, how ungrateful it would be
to admit that we didn't love each other after all this.

Jason worried and chewed his fingernails until the cuticles
bled. I worried, too. Jason had been so smooth with me at
first, and when it turned out that he wasn't smooth at all,

that was both endearing and frightening. His confusion made me feel sick. He knew he belonged with his children and his parents and he hated me because he loved me and that hurt them. He didn't want to hurt them. He thought his stomach aches were cancer. He couldn't sleep. Nothing I did could please him.

That was the beginning.

chapter 3

Handel's *Water Music*. Through a soft-focus lens we see a long white strand of beach at twilight. On a bluff in the foreground is an old-fashioned gray shingled summer house with green trim and shutters. Seagulls wheel and call out above it. The last rays of a fluffy gold and pink sunset streak the evening sky. The sea is calm tonight, small waves lap the beach.

In the distance, two figures walk toward the house, and as they come closer they take the form of a man and a woman, wandering slowly down the beach holding hands. The skirts of her flowered summer dress shift around her in the breeze, she lifts it to walk in the water up to her ankles, then drops it when she comes back onto the sand. She is tanned and her light brown hair, bleached out by the sun, blows across her face. The man is tall, blond and tanned too, and he has rolled his white pants up around his knees to splash in the shallows at the tideline. As they reach the dunes just below the house he puts his arm around her and they are laughing and hugging each other as they scramble up the bluff in the dark.

We had gone up to Nantucket to open the Gardens' cottage there the summer after we were married. The wounds of the wedding had almost healed, the sky sparkled in the sun. The first day we took down the shutters and swept out the rooms. Jason patched a leak in the south dormer and I helped him caulk the old wooden boat in the garage. Later I sorted the linen, cool folds of sheets and towels neatly stacked and monogrammed and smelling faintly of lavender. Jason's mother liked everything just so.

The next day was ours and Jason decided to make clam chowder from scratch. Really from scratch. We put on our bathing suits—I had a blue and white bikini that year—and T-shirts and, with Jason carrying an empty bushel basket and me the picnic lunch, we headed up the beach toward Coskata Pond. Coskata is really an inland lake in the center of a narrow spit of land that divides the Atlantic Ocean and the inner harbor. It is surrounded by salt marshes and connected to the harbor by a shallow creek. As we got near the pond, sea birds and ducks flew off above us and rabbits scurried away through the scrub pine. Jason showed me the white shape of a heron, standing on one leg at the other side of the water.

Odd work. For quahogs you bend over at the waist and drag your heels backward through the sand in shallow water. Wiggle your hips and concentrate all sensation on the backs of your feet. Then suddenly, with a hollow heavy feeling your heel hits a buried quahog about three inches down in the sand and you turn around and scoop it out of the water, the heavy shell lying like a wet round stone in your hand. Steamers are more difficult to find. You walk along the shore looking for tiny holes and when you find one, jump with one foot on each side of the hole. If it squirts, you kneel over the hole and dig like mad. Steamers can dig very fast, their long necks pulling them deep into the sand, and they are a great prize.

Jason had packed a picnic of cold zucchini and thick ham sandwiches with mustard on crusty bread from the Portuguese bakery and after we filled the bushel basket with quahogs we walked over to the ocean for a swim and then sat in the shade and had lunch. Cool white wine. We talked about how nice it would be to have a dog. And afterward we walked home down the creek that joins Coskata to the bay. Jason showed me the markings of the sandpipers who scooted away from us and we found a scallop at the water's edge opening and shutting with its tiny bright blue eyes in each indentation of the shell.

I was walking behind Jason when he stopped suddenly and pointed and in the water I could see two blue crabs, with brilliant backs, sidling along in the sand. As we watched, frozen still, they both stood up on their side legs and danced a mating dance right there in the middle of the creek. They kicked up little plumes of sand and the sun warmed our backs and the creek cooled our feet and the crabs danced and I was as happy as I had ever been. The happiest I've been. Gentle Jason. Jason knew everything about the sea and its creatures.

On the beach at the cove below the house he showed me the long thin tracks of the black crescent horseshoe crab, an ancient animal. We turned one over and its skinny feet clawed wildly at the air and then we found a baby horseshoe crab with a translucent pale brown shell.

Later we made the chowder in the old high-ceilinged kitchen that a whaler built to console his wife until he came back from the sea. I fried the salt pork and then the onions in the heavy cast-iron frying pan and Jason did the rest and when the chowder was simmering and the biscuits were ready for the oven we went back out and walked up the beach and then we came back and had a summer feast of the chowder, thick with cream and the succulent quahogs, and hot biscuits with fresh butter spilling over them. Cool white wine and strong coffee in little blue cups.

And then, burping and laughing, we went back out on the nighttime sand. Beach in the moonlight, the silver throwing strange shadows on the dunes, the surface of the water black and mysterious and scary. And we walked up along the ocean side and Jason took off his blue Shetland sweater and put it down on the sand in a hollow between two dunes and we sat on it and then he made love to me. Quick and sweet. This was Jason's place and he was in control—and he was beautiful. I thought he knew everything in those days, everything about birds and animals and food and houses and women. And he wanted to share it with me. And he was so sure.

chapter 4

My father's family came from Boston, Massachusetts. And even in that tight-lipped society, the Potters were notorious for their profligate and eccentric way of life. My Great-Aunt Sarah, a determined and bony woman with a crown of dark braids, starved herself to death in the Potter family house at Braintree to protest the famine in Pakistan. In his eighties, doddering Great-Uncle Edward frequently had to be fished out of Boston Harbor where he insisted on sailing the leaky ancestral catboat each Sunday in pursuit, as he explained to the Coast Guard, of the varieties of religious experience. His daughter, Abigail, was a devoted follower of the Swami Krishna Maha and she eventually sold everything she had and went to live in a commune near Bangalore. Even my grandfather was a well-known character who used to appear on sunny afternoons in the Public Garden to declaim Shakespeare to the swans.

My father, although he treasured his own eccentricities,

was not amused. To him, the colorful Potter history was a saga of self-indulgence and weakness, and the Potter family stories that I loved hearing were always told by more distant relatives—my grandmother, Great-Uncle Jim, or Uncle Albert.

My father's older brother, Albert, had been a golden boy at school—one of those young men whose talents and charm seem to have no limits—and after Milton and Harvard he had married a very pretty girl and taken a promising job on the administrative side of Boyle and Cunningham Shipping Agents. But ordinary life didn't suit Uncle Albert. He was a charming failure as a businessman, a passable failure as the publisher of a small boating magazine, a barely acceptable failure as a yacht broker, and a drunken and embarrassing failure as a salesman for *Encyclopaedia Britannica*. My father, who had methodically parlayed his own and my mother's inheritances into a comfortable fortune, often let his disdain for Albert's improvidence show through the polite veneer of brotherly love.

"What can you do with a man like that?" he would say, writing a check to cover some new debt or other that Albert had run up and couldn't pay.

I loved Uncle Albert. His pockets were always filled with Keene's Curiously Strong Peppermints, he had an unending store of jokes and card tricks to share, and he never stopped telling a bedtime story before you fell asleep. Once, when I was older and home from school for the summer, I ran into him by accident on Madison Avenue; his visits to my parents had become rarer and rarer and I hadn't even known he was in New York. It was one of those sweltering August days in the city when everything seems to sweat and smell.

"We'll go have a nice cool drink at the Stanhope," he said, greeting me with an avuncular kiss, "but first I'll show you something even cooler."

He guided me down Seventieth Street to the Frick Museum and we passed out of the glare of the sun through the dim foyer to the inner courtyard where fountains splashed among the indoor greenery. At first I thought that was our destination, but Uncle Albert hurried past the fountains without stopping and I followed him into the dark recesses of the old mansion's West Wing. He was standing absolutely still in the corner room in front of the John Constable oil painting of Salisbury Cathedral. In the green distance of that faraway place a fat cow stood cooling in a shallow stream and the stones of the Cathedral glowed golden. High trees threw late afternoon shadows on the broad meadow. The heat and the New York streets were hundreds of years and thousands of miles away.

"Oh, Constable," my father said when I got home. "He was never anything but a second-rate academic."

I can see now that my father was annoyed by my fascination with Albert; I can even sympathize with his fears that I would be infected by the sad craziness in my own blood, and with his insistence that I be brought up by the rules. But at the time I couldn't understand this, because my father seemed so sure of himself, so totally invincible, so irrevocably solid. His shoulders smelled of whiskey and old tweed, and burying my little girl's face in the slightly scratchy surface of his jacket, I felt completely safe. Once, when I was about ten, we took a family ski trip to Woodstock, Vermont, and somehow my clothes got inextricably tangled in the rope tow. It was only at the last minute that my father, straddling the ruts of the primitive tow line, was able to free me. But what I remember most clearly about that ride up toward the deadly, clanking machinery of the tow was that in spite of my mother's screams, I was completely unafraid. My father was there and there was nothing to worry about. He would be able to free me, I knew, and he did.

As far as I could tell my mother felt the same way about him. I loved hearing the stories of their long-ago courtship at Columbia with its amusing ups and downs all leading to one wonderful and inevitable result—me. My father had been a distinguished man even then, and so after some initial objections, my mother's family consented and she received her father's blessing and her trust fund on schedule.

I'm not at all sure where they first met Jason's parents although I know it was before either of us was born. It could have been at Columbia, or through New York friends, or even at Illyria, a baronial estate on the Hudson that had been turned into a working colony for writers and scholars. Anyway, I guess you could say I have known Jason's parents all my life although I didn't meet *him* until much later. For a while before I was born, my parents and the Gardens lived in the same brick pre-war apartment building on the Upper West Side near the university. My parents had a two-bedroom apartment with views of the river and the New Jersey Palisades, and the Gardens had a smaller apartment on the inside. After Jason was born, my parents even baby sat for him sometimes. They enjoyed it, they said. It was a nice way of preparing for the child they were looking forward to having themselves.

chapter 5

If I had known Jason earlier, I suppose, everything might have been different. But by the time we met I was no longer a child and I was sure that I had outgrown my parents' influence. I had graduated from college and I held a salaried job in a faraway state. I had gone to Mississippi and Alabama to help save the world in the civil rights days of the 1960s—over my father's protests. I had been in love with many men; and I had made love to two of them.

The first was a handsome fellow freshman named Ned Winthrop, or perhaps I loved his fine bones and his upperclass manner and his family who lived in Boston, Massachusetts. Ned's grandfather had built the Wadsworth Atheneum, but we spent stolen nights together in a Back Bay tenement off Symphony Road. The walls were thin and the man next door coughed all night. "This is happiness," I thought as I lay next to Ned's slim body. "This is it."

In those days, sex was accomplished by small increments

over a period of weeks or even months. But in our first springtime passion Ned and I had spent some hungry hours together on the grass below Memorial Drive, and when I went back to New York that summer to my college-girl job at *Time* Magazine, birth control was very much on my mind.

A friend in the office who was having an affair with the Sports Editor told me what to do.

I went to Lamston's and chose a diamond ring out of a tray next to the nail polish counter. I made up a wedding date and an address, and at lunch hour on Thursday I took the bus uptown to the Planned Parenthood office on the Upper West Side. After a long wait in an outer office, a motherly gray-haired woman ushered me down the hall into a drab room with two camp chairs and a desk. She watched carefully as I filled out a long form with my false name, my false address, and the false date of our false wedding-to-be. I was ablaze with embarrassment and fear and kept my head down so that she couldn't see my face. Halfway through the form, though, she started to ask questions.

"I'm afraid it's against our policy," she said, her face suddenly closed. "Unless you have something to show that you really *are* getting married."

I walked home through the park. What could I do? She was right, after all. Good girls got married. In the end, after a tearful scene and much explanation, I was able to persuade a friend's gynecologist to fit me for a diaphragm, but that moment at Planned Parenthood stayed with me.

Months later, back in Cambridge, I went up to the Dean of Women's office in Bradford Hall to ask about getting a job after I graduated. I had decided I wanted to be a reporter.

"What does a girl like you want a job for?" asked Dean

Abigail White, smoothing her beige suit across her impecca-
ble lap. "All our *best* girls are engaged."

There was something about the way she said it. Ned was
waiting for me in the sun outdoors. We walked across the
quadrangle toward the dormitories.

"Why don't we get engaged?" I asked him.

"Are you kidding?" he said.

I started to cry. We walked past the dormitories and
through Cambridge down to the banks of the Charles. I
wept.

"Okay, okay, we're engaged," he said.

I don't remember much about sex with Ned, sexual memories fade so fast. But it always had a delicious, secret
I-shouldn't-be-doing-this-but-I-can't-help-myself feeling. It
started one summer weekend when we were sent up the
coast to his family's summer house to deliver a new mast for
the boat.

"Whatever you do, please don't spend the night," his
mother said, as we tied the mast to the top of the car.

We spent the night. We had been in love for months, but
we didn't know how to make love. We lay there on the bed
in that summer cottage on a hill above Penobscot Bay and
pressed our bodies together. I could feel the stiffness of
Ned's cock against me as he undressed me. But he was
afraid, too. He gently spread my thighs and fit himself to
them, rubbing this hard shaft of flesh back and forth between my legs until he came. I belonged to him that night,
he could have done anything. There were other times like
that too: with our hands on his parents' sofa while we
watched television, and then one night in the guest bedroom
he finally guided himself inside me.

"No," I said, "no, Ned." (That was what we said in those
days when we meant yes.)

But he was there already, breaking into me, having me

with strange sounding moaning cries. Later in the bathroom I noticed that there was blood on my thighs.

There was a winter after that summer. We ate a lot of cheap hamburger. We went everywhere together. We were in love. It was the summer after that that the whole thing began to fall apart. I was living in a dingy apartment behind the college with three other girls and he was living in his parents' big house on Linnean Street. His mother had never forgiven me. I was lonely. Through the wall of my bedroom at night I would hear one of my housemates and her boyfriend. The animal noises, the rhythmic creak of the cheap bed. Ned never spent the night.

"I guess you don't even care enough about me to spend the night in a dreary house," I said. He was silent. Then one morning I went to see him, there had been a light rain and the late summer air smelled of the Winthrops' well-kept lawn. He was upstairs when I found him, listening to his collection of baroque flute records.

"Let's go downstairs," he said.

We went back down to the kitchen and he opened the refrigerator door and took out a can of Mott's tomato juice. A note was Scotch-taped to the white refrigerator door. "Take Danny to the Dr./Get milk/P.T.A. meet. Tues." Ned poured the thick red liquid into a heavy green juice glass.

"It's over," he said.

He was right.

That night I cried my eyes out in the arms of his temporary replacement, a weak-chinned summer-school student named Peter who had been asking me to go to the movies with him for a month.

"There, there, Salley," he said, holding me on the bed of his apartment at the back of a house on Brooke Street, stroking me as close to my breasts and thighs as he dared under the circumstances. The rain was falling in earnest now, coming in sheets past the windows and gurgling down the rusty gutters and making the city shine in the streetlights.

But the next one was Harry, and that was a year later. He was the captain of the Oberlin College tennis team and I met him in Alabama.

I did a lot of civil rights work that summer, and again the summer I graduated, and I found out that civil rights work meant all kinds of things. The waiting room at the grimy Jackson airport. The thrill of adventure and the metallic taste of fear. Heart pounding, bowels loose, crouching in the back of a green pickup truck on a bumpy dirt road in Philadelphia County at night while the Sheriff shone his spotlight in at the driver's seat.

"No sir, there's no one in the back, sir."

And scuffing up the dust on the country roads around Shubuta, living on sweet bubbly grape soda from cool machines in the old wooden gas stations. Skin burned from the noontime Mississippi sun. House after house, creaking steps and rickety porches with the dogs barking and the children running for their parents and then the hard slam of the screen door.

"Go away, we don't want your kind here."

For a while I slept on a bookshelf in the back of an old building on the Meridian Highway in Quitman. That was the worst time, and I didn't stay for long. We had a lot of guns, but none of us really knew how to use them. In the beginning, we had had the whole building for the Organization. "Headquarters Building" we called it grandly in our dispatches to Jackson. But slowly, as the dream faded, the two old black people who took care of the building for its liberal white owner let us have less and less of it. Finally all five of us were living in that cramped back room and sleeping on the bookshelves. With the guns. And one night after crazy Bill T. had been snooping around the Quitman police

station and they shot at him to scare him, he thought it
would be a fine joke to paint a white target on the plate-glass
windows in front of the building. We all laughed. It seemed
funny.

But later that night as I wandered out for air across the
scrawny weeds of the vacant lot next door, I saw those two
old black people out with their pails and brushes by the
flickering streetlights erasing Bill's joke. Bending and scrubbing, bending and scrubbing. They didn't think it was
funny. I felt sick. These were the people we had come to
help and they just wanted us to go away; they all wanted us
to go away. And I did go away.

But Alabama wasn't like that at all. I was at Tuskegee,
registering voters with a group of other white kids from
Northern colleges. We played a lot of tennis, had barbecues
twice a week, and went to the movies in Montgomery. I
lived in one of the college dormitories and my roommate
was a black girl named Georgia Washington. I thought we
were friends, and she had a friend named Sammy Young, a
scrawny handsome boy who came around to watch us play
tennis sometimes.

Each Tuesday evening the leader of our group, a wealthy
do-gooder from New Canaan, Connecticut, summoned us to
a meeting where we would earnestly compare notes and
progress.

Sammy Young made fun of our meetings.

"If you want to see a real meeting you should come to the
SNCC meetings," he would say. But he would never tell me
where they were or when. Once I saw him standing at the
corner of Bibb Street handing out notices for a meeting but
when he saw me coming he laughed and held them up out
of my reach.

We didn't know then what was going to happen. We
didn't know they were going to shoot Sammy Young. Or

that the county would be redistricted so that the voters we registered didn't make any difference. We didn't know, and Harry and I used to walk around the Tuskegee campus holding hands as if we were back at Radcliffe or Oberlin.

"I don't know why you let me do this to you," he would say, after I let him pull my underpants off and my skirt up and do everything he wanted in the grass under the pine trees above the tennis courts where we used to go at night. "I'm not going to marry you."

He was a doctor's son and his family lived in a big house with columns on Green Farms Road about ten miles from our house in Connecticut. In the fall we made love behind his parents' house in the soft grass and pine needles under those northern firs.

"Sex is so wonderful," he would say, tossing the sagging condom into the woods.

A very nice guy, Harry.

Later, when I came back from Mississippi, he came to see me at my parents' house. I fell asleep while he was telling me about a girl he had met in the Bennington library. I had forgotten my diaphragm. He had forgotten his condoms. He went back to his elegant house and I never saw him again.

chapter 6

Erik Erikson says that marriages made in the early twenties are inevitably part of the couple's relationship with their respective parents. You want to break free, but you want to be taken care of. You want to please them, but you want to show them who's boss now. And when I finally met Jason, during the month of July when I had come back to New York on vacation from Laramie, he seemed to offer me all these things. It was at an Independence Day party in a professor's apartment near Columbia, a few blocks from the building where our parents had once lived together. In fact, we had heard so much about each other that our meeting seemed like a joke between old friends.

"Oh, yes," I laughed, "Jason Gardens."

He was older than I was and part of another world. An Eastern, New York City world of jobs with offices and secretaries and lunches in restaurants with red banquettes. Norman Mailer had taught him how to box. Gregory Corso had written a poem about him. He had gone to Yale, but he looked more like Princeton, tall and sleek with carefully combed blond hair, a gaunt face partly hidden by big horn-rimmed glasses and a tone of voice so polite that it was sometimes hard to tell if he was being deferential or ironic.

Jason had troubles too, as I found out over dinner. A first wife who had slept with his best friend. (A man big enough to admit that he had been hurt.) Two little daughters whom he saw on weekends and worried about the rest of the time. (A man with a heart, a father.) A serious nervous break-down in his last year at college, which had left him with a fear of heights and a romantic hypochondria. And, best of all, an overwhelming desire to find the right girl, chuck all this New York silliness and go off to a Vermont farmhouse to cook, grow his own vegetables, and write the novel he knew he had in him.

We had a rocky first month. He was infatuated in his smooth way, and I told myself I was just playing along with it. Jason was as good a way to pass a pleasant month as any. But then, just as I decided it would be amusing if he pro-posed—then he withdrew.

"I'm coming downtown tonight," I said one morning as we drank our coffee in bed. "Gonnabearound?"

"Actually, I'm not," he said. A little laugh. A little hug, the knife.

There was a wonderful weekend just before I left to go back to Laramie. I had gone off for a few days with another man, an old friend, and this had given Jason the impression that I was powerful and didn't need him and it made him want me. His withdrawal had given me the same impression about him. We spoke very little those two golden days. We were tough and in love. And when it was time for me to go back I realized that he didn't want me to leave.

Three weeks later, after an exchange of witty and noncommittal letters, he called me and asked me to marry him.

In the end, how could I resist? Jason was older and taller and experienced. He had already been married and he knew about it. A man of the world. A graduate of Yale and Austen Riggs. He would help me break away from this career going nowhere on a nothing Laramie paper, and he would take care of me in style. When I said with a giggle on our third date that I wasn't sure I should sleep with him, he had answered with assurance:

"You will."

And I did.

And when I said later that I wasn't sure if I should marry him, he had answered in that same way:

"You will."

Then the minister shall say unto the woman,

Salley, wilt thou have this man to thy wedded husband, to live together after God's ordinance in the holy estate of Matrimony? Wilt thou love him, comfort him, honour, and keep him in sickness and in health; and, forsaking all others, keep thee only unto him, so long as ye both shall live?

The woman shall answer,

I will.

And after that I was no longer C— average Salley Potter who could never get into a club at Miss Singer's and hid in the ladies room at the Christmas dances. No siree. I was Mrs. Jason Gardens, the wife of Jason Gardens of Exeter and Yale and New York City. I got wedding presents. I got respect from salesladies and from other people's mothers. I even got two hundred vellum cards that said "Mrs. Jason Gardens."

Not that it's been that bad. It's certainly not Jason's fault that I am such a fool. Nor that I thought at first his craziness was so romantic, or that if two people loved each other nothing else mattered. It's enough for Jason just to keep himself together at all, just to get through life without bringing the disaster he sees everywhere down on his handsome head. He can barely get by, and he certainly can't afford to take chances.

There is a mean joke I tease him with these days. When the Grim Reaper finally comes for Jason, I tell him, that skeletal spook coming to take him forever away from the joys of life and the flesh and feelings, Jason will say:

"Phew, I made it."

chapter 7

In this city, sometimes, when you go around a corner or reach the top of a hill the Bay suddenly opens out before you. The island of Alcatraz squats in the water with its angular white cement buildings. You can see a few sails, and then the smooth hills of Marin County in the distance beyond the Golden Gate. In the winter the hills are brown; in the summer they are green. The water is always blue. San Francisco blues.

Our apartment is in the back through a paved alleyway lined with plants. There are white latticework shutters on the windows and a deck outside the bedroom with an old-fashioned bolt lock on the door like the one on the boathouse in New Hampshire. Jason has built a crude railing around the deck so that Valdi, the little dachshund we bought in London, can safely bask in the sun. The planks are worn wood with ivy growing up through them and from the deck you can see three backyards, the tower of Lone

Mountain College in the distance and beyond that a Sears and Bekins Company sign that flashes on and off at night and the high domed roof of the Lake Street Synagogue. I write all this down so that I will remember it, because I seem to have forgotten so many details of the recent past. Five years of married life are telescoped into a few images: the white clapboard house on the Hudson where we lived when we left New York City; the flat on Egerton Crescent that we rented for the year we were in London, where Jason worked on the magazine's British counterpart; the gray shingled summer place where we spent a Nantucket weekend.

Jason says that the best view around here is the view from Annie's back door. Annie lives in an old white farmhouse with blue trim and lots of angles and a peaked roof with dormers. Once it dominated the surrounding fields of hay and corn and pumpkins, but now the fertile Berkeley soil grows highrises, boxy pink stucco apartments, and the four-lane neon-lighted strip of University Avenue. Annie's moldings are painted mustard yellow, the same color we had in our room at college, but then there is a little wooden porch with a rickety roof and a back vegetable garden with squash and morning glory vines trailing in the grass. Annie came here one day with nothing but a trunkful of books, and now she agonizes over what she will do when she finally gets her doctorate in the spring.

"It's terrible to have the future hanging over your head," she complains. We have renewed our old friendship and we drink tea on the cushions in her study, the desk piled high with papers and notebooks.

It's worse not to have anything hanging over your head, I think.

They hang very loose here. When it rains everything leaks and you can almost always hear through the walls even in the most expensive apartments. When you walk through the residential streets above the Bay, Pacific Heights, and look into the windows of the grand houses, the ornate Victorian fantasies of the silver barons, there are never any families sitting around the dinner table or people reading to their children or sitting in a book-lined study in a wing chair under the lamp. Instead there are huge house-plants in ceramic pots and blank modern paintings. Empty rooms with Saarinen chairs and Breuer tables. Sometimes a dog barks.

We are here for a reason. Jason was restless at the maga-zine after we came back from London, and now he and Gerry Black have quit together and come to San Francisco to work as editors on the *Saturday Review*. O ho, the *Satur-day Review*, you say. Yes, there were many promises made, there were dinners at Quo Vadis and lunches at La Cara-velle. There was talk about a publishing empire and con-dominiums at Squaw Valley and chartering jets, and with the money they gave Jason we paid all our debts. We tore the last twelve coupons out of the car payment book and sent them off to Chase Manhattan with a check. We were a little afraid, but they were so sure.

There were two of them.

"Soon, the *Saturday Review* will be an empire," Rosen-crantz promised us.

"A talented contributor like Jason will be able to do any-thing he wants, books, travel, perhaps even his own maga-zine," added Guildenstern.

"We've hired Christopher Eliot-Smith away from the *Times* to be our book man," said Rosencrantz. "We took him out to lunch at Lutèce last week and signed him up. His first review will appear in ten days."

"What if it stinks?" said Guildenstern. (Rosencrantz was the intellectual.)

"Then we'll take him back to Lutèce and fire him," said Rosencrantz.

It certainly wasn't their fault that we were all such fools. But by the time we got to San Francisco the empire was already in disarray, and at the opening party in the new building—a remodeled tuna-canning factory with bare brick walls and brightly painted utility pipes—most people anxiously discussed ways to get back East.

It wasn't so funny. Jason couldn't sleep.

The day we moved into our apartment, Rosencrantz told him that we might have to move out.

Late on an overcast Saturday afternoon, Jason had a private meeting with Guildenstern in an imitation English Pub near Fisherman's Wharf. When I went to meet Jason afterwards, I saw him coming up Sacramento Street eating a green apple. Later he said, "I bought the apple and I ate it slowly because I knew if you saw me eating an apple you would know I was okay."

But he wasn't at all okay.

There was another meeting in a rented house on the muddy slopes that veer into the sea above Bolinas. Plywood and glass. After dinner, the editors, who were all men, went down to the den, and the editors' wives, who were all women, stayed in the shag-carpeted living room perched uncomfortably on the modern chairs and sofas. The house and everything in it seemed temporary, a waystop, nobody's real home, and we all wished like hell we were somewhere else while the murmur of our fate being decided filtered up from downstairs.

As soon as the men left, our hostess went to the kitchen for a can of Lemon Pledge and began to wipe the rings off the coffee tables, empty the ashtrays and plump up the pillows where the men had been. She was a small, pale woman who seemed to reflect the tenseness of that evening and, as she dusted the chair next to me, I noticed that her red-polished fingernails were bitten to the quick. Later, hours later, because the men didn't come upstairs until almost dawn, she began to talk to us about her childhood. Balanced like a bird on the edge of a chair, her bubble of brown hair bobbing back and forth, she told us about growing up in the slums outside Chicago and her family living in two rooms and having to go to work at sixteen, and by the end of the story she was sobbing and hugging herself in distress.

"I never wanted to come here," she sobbed. "I never wanted to come here."

Mutual, lady.

When it rains in San Francisco it is cold and gray and the water streaks against the windows and you can see it falling heavily outdoors. There are no cloudbursts, just a heavy wall of water that forms crystal drops on the accordion-shaped metal fire escapes and the elaborate wooden cornices and makes the painted shingles sweat and darken.

I go to see Kim Kavy on a rainy day in January. He is the head of a local television station. I am looking for work. While I wait for him, I rehearse my spiel. Two years as a reporter on the Laramie *Eagle*. Six months as a writer for the BBC in London. One Associated Press award. A career truncated by marriage, I'm afraid. You know how it is. Heh, heh.

Kim Kavy sits in a swivel chair at the back of the newsroom. I tell him that I have sent my resumé to his personnel department. He nods. He opens a manila folder on his desk and dumps out ten resumés. Mine is at the bottom. He wears a green corduroy shirt and a frayed jacket and his high forehead shows through thinning hair. Through the thick lenses of his glasses I catch an expression that means he doesn't think that there is really any point in talking to me. Why am I there?

"Even if I had a position open now, you . . ." his voice trails off.

He tells me that he is looking for a black reporter. He tells me that he knows he shouldn't tell me that he is looking for a black reporter.

He picks up another resumé, the one on top. "There are lots of good people around town looking for work," he says. "Here's Andrea Swamps, a girl with real television experience, a well-known name out here."

I feel invisible. He lolls back in his swivel chair and eyes me blankly. His balls bulge out through his double-knit trousers and he reaches down to scratch them absentmindedly. He tells me what a great reporter he was when he first came to San Francisco to work for *Newsweek*.

"The other guys out here didn't know dogshit about what was going on," he says. He smiles for the first time.

The interview is over.

I don't feel right again until I am back in the car and fifteen blocks away at Franklin and Pine with the radio blasting rock on my way home.

At Squaw Valley the aerial tramway is painted turquoise and pink with pink leatherette trim. Inside, a whole family carries skis that have ECOLOGY printed on them in big green and white letters. The children all have braces on their teeth. Jason clenches his jaw as we are swept up the mountain through the snow, trees and rock ledges receding below us. He is afraid.

They say that Squaw Valley is the place where the women and children stayed when the braves went off to hunt. The Valley of the Squaws. How come they get to do all the hunting while we stay in this valley with the cooking and the teepeework? How come they get to be called braves? My mind is gummed up like an old engine. Seized.

At cocktail parties we go to I tell people that I don't know if I am gestating or vegetating. They laugh. I should buy sheets, I should do the marketing, I should call Barbara Black and ask the Blacks to dinner, I should take out the garbage, vacuum the floor, brush Valdi, write letters applying for jobs. Instead, I eat an apple.

In California the gas they use in the death chamber smells like peaches. Strange fruit. Holding your breath until your lungs sting and ache and your eyes bulge out and you think you will burst. This can't be happening to me. Then the final sucking in. Relief, air, poison. Why don't they give you a choice of flavors?

Driving. The Golden Gate Bridge stretches like an iron bracelet across the Bay. A rainbow is painted on the arched entrance of the tunnel to Sausalito. The hills look like a green carpet that someone has dropped over the peaks and chasms of the rocky coastline. You are the sunshine of my life. The rainwashed landscape of greens and blues in this sparkling air, the Bay all blue and glittering in the sun, and the city with towers clean and white stacked together like children's blocks.

They talk a lot about ecology here, but in the little villages along the northern coast there is no money for new-fangled sewage systems and so you can't swim in the Pacific above Stinson Beach because it's polluted. At Point Reyes there are signs warning you not to touch the seals because they are polluted, too. There are ecology T-shirts and ecology clinics and ecology workshops and ecology shopping bags, but the factories in Oakland across the Bay belch their wastes into the clear winter skies. Oil shimmers on the rocks below the Golden Gate. Conservation is for conversation.

"Ecology? Oh, are you interested in ecology? Well, I am extremely interested in ecology myself. Let's fuck."

I am standing in the Van Ness Avenue Post Office waiting

to mail off a stack of job applications when a blind girl comes up behind me in the line. She has short-cropped hair and pimples on her cheeks and chin. She is overweight and sort of carelessly dressed the way blind people often are because they can't see, and she holds out her white cane with dirty hands. I am terrified.

She has that eager, friendly, peering through the darkness look of the blind. How lucky I am after all, I think, trying not to touch her, making myself small, making an effort not to bolt. Do the blind sense these things?

"It's all right, you're doing fine, you're next in the line," I croon when she bumps into me—as if she were the frightened animal instead of me. My hackles bristle.

"You sound like a very gentle person," she says. "My name is Linda."

"I'm just tired of waiting in line," I say.

The blind girl who sat next to me in Latin class at Miss Singer's School was named Mary. She had delicate features and wavy soft blond hair and she was a Swanson from Philadelphia, but at the center of her blue eyes there was a blank where the pupil should have been. Everyone liked Mary at school, everyone helped to take care of her. And when they saw us in our blue serge uniforms with knee socks and oxfords helping Mary up the path to the dormitory or down the hall to the cafeteria, the teachers at Miss Singer's nodded with satisfaction.

"Our girls are learning compassion," they said to each other.

But their girls had a lot to learn. I arrived there in the fall of the year I was thirteen, too plump and too smart to be popular, and in the three years I spent in that Victorian stone pile with its grand trees and grassy park I got plumper and smarter and even less popular. The first week was typical. The entire school was permanently divided into two teams, the Betas and the Gammas, and after three days of intense physical competitions in which my adolescent lack of coordination was painfully apparent, the ceremony of assigning each new girl to her team was held on the west lawn.

One by one we walked down an aisle, a gauntlet, between the two teams of upperclasswomen, trying to look athletic and brave, and pulled a little tab out of a silver chalice that had been used for the same purpose since the school was founded in 1846.

"She's a Beta!" the girl holding the chalice would shout if the paper you pulled out of the chalice was red, or, if it was blue, "She's a Gamma!"

The girls on each team cheered wildly when a pretty or athletic blond pulled out their team color, and they booed in angry disappointment if any uncoordinated and plump brunette was assigned to them by chance.

When I became a Beta—"She's a Beta!"—there was a moment of ominous silence and then the captain of the Betas, a tall senior with blond braids and a lithe body, stood up at the back of the crowd and pointed her index finger at her head like a gun and fell back on the grass as if in a faint. Everyone laughed.

The school was also divided by class, by dormitory, by teacher-counselor, and by clubs. It was the clubs that finally drove me to hide in the Chapel on the top floor of the school for three days. And after that Miss Louise Underwood, the headmistress, wrote to my parents to suggest that I might be happier at some other school.

Each club had a special jacket, its symbol of prestige. The literary club jacket was a tartan plaid, and the drama club jacket a pale beige, and the athletic club jacket was green with a white shield on the pocket. Everyone else wore the blue serge jacket that went with the school uniform. Each spring the whole school was herded into the gymnasium and the jacketed members of each club silently and solemnly wove through the crowd in a line. For each girl who had been voted into the club through secret ballot the night before there was a scream and her name was called out and the girl at the head of the line leaped on her and everyone crowded around with hugs and congratulations. A jacket was draped over her shoulders and she joined the solemn procession. I would watch them from the bleachers above the gym. The silence and the scream and everyone shouting and then the new club member, blubbering and sobbing with joy, her arms around her new colleagues, joining this exclusive minuet.

Years later I was at a party at Elaine's in New York and I met a girl who had been a class ahead of me at Miss Singer's. She was a successful playwright who had become notorious for pushiness and ambition, and I was a journalist then. We joked merrily about the fact that, back at Miss Singer's, she hadn't been elected to the Drama Club and I hadn't been elected to the Literary Club, while most of the girls who had been elected had long since married bankers and stockbrokers and faded into the social woodwork of the Main Line or Chestnut Hill or Grosse Pointe. She told me that she had recently gone back to Miss Singer's at Miss Louise Underwood's invitation to talk to the girls about her successful career. And when one of them asked where she had found the stamina and the drive to make such a success for herself so quickly, she said:

"Well, I guess I'm just still trying to get my jacket."

chapter 8

It's Christmas in San Francisco, but the flower stalls are spilling over with pungent roses and carnations and the grass is velvety green under the palms in Union Square. In Gump's, four carolers in nineteenth-century bustles and bonnets wander among the Oriental vases and ivory *objets* singing "Good King Wenceslas." At the corner a burly black man with a German shepherd in a worn-out dog sweater lying beside him begs in a growly voice. Oh yes, can you spare a dime, sir? But the air is filled with the warmth and fragrance of early spring, the carolers and the German shepherd are too hot in their winter clothes, and there is no falling snow for King Wenceslas to leave his saintly prints in. Christmas in California. Was the manger organic? Was the Christ child a Lamaze baby? Did the Virgin Mother remember to take her kelp and Vitamin A pills? Did they have one thing from each of the essential food groups at the Last Supper?

A housewife's work expands to fill the time allowed. I should be vacuuming (Valdi is shedding his winter coat in this warm weather), changing the sheets, putting leftover côte de veau a la Nivernaise in a smaller pot and washing the big pot, calling the *San Francisco Examiner* to ask if they will interview me for a job.

But they've just hired a woman, what would they want with another one? I can hear them saying it. Especially one who puts off doing the vacuuming.

I go to see Mel Pearman, an editor at the *San Francisco Chronicle*. They say he is a terror. Instead he is a dapper little man who wears striped suspenders and has a silk handkerchief tucked in the pocket of his suit jacket. He sits at the front of a large city room that looks like all other city rooms. Ranks of gray, middle-aged men, some talking on the telephone, some typing, some just sitting there numbed by the constant droning of each other's voices. Pearman and I talk about restaurants in France. He and his wife have just spent a month on the Tour Gastronomique, he tells me. Illhaeusern, Mionnay, Eugénie-les-Bains. I think about indigestion. I try to impress him with my French accent, my sophistication, my knowledge of European food. Later I realize this was a terrible mistake. I never quite understand why. No jobs, I'm sorry but there are no jobs now. There are never any jobs now.

Haim Ginott says that you should never give a child an order without providing some alternative because you will violate the child's autonomy. Right. Violate my autonomy. I'll really still respect you afterward if you'll just let me violate your autonomy just this one time. Please. Violet your geranium. Christmas is a week away, a week away, a week away. Salley's mad song. Keep the dog from hence that's friend to man, they shed on the carpets and you have to vacuum every day. An old woman's cackle. The voices coming through the wall from the next apartment violate my autonomy. Giving dinner parties for Jason's piggy colleagues violates my autonomy. Following Jason wherever his professional ambitions take him violates my autonomy.

"You can be a goddamned sight more accommodating," he said last night, leaning against the corner of the front hall with the tweed cap from England on his head and his sheepskin coat hanging open. We didn't make love and this morning I noticed that the bottle of Scotch was gone.

One morning I wake up and I can hear Jason in the kitchen.

"Christ, ants!" he says in an aggravated voice. The coarse sound of insect spray. Later, after he has left for work, I go into the kitchen and find dozens of dead ants on and around the dog food bag. Inside the bag the ants are chewing and swarming over the dry brown chunks and I have to throw the whole thing out. I clean up the dead ants and add dog food to the marketing list.

I feel invisible here. Sometimes I think if you aren't wearing the California Girl uniform—faded jeans and a T-shirt, clogs and long straight hair—you don't really exist. No one looks at you. When we were living with Barbara and Gerry Black after we first came I used to walk down to Union Street for lunch sometimes. Barbara was very unhappy then and the children were always crying and I'd flee, driving down to the marina and parking the little rented car and wandering through the strange bright streets in my neat little Banlon dresses with my matching high-heeled sandals and handbag. No one looked. No one smiled. I used to eat sometimes in a restaurant called "The Natural Thing" where you got a sandwich that was mostly alfalfa sprouts on crumbly brown bread and a piece of fruit and you could dawdle over it in a dark corner and read—or just give yourself over to daydreaming and wishing you had somewhere else to go. Once, an older man in blue jeans came in and sat down at the next table. We were alone back there. Look at me, please, I willed him. Try to start a conversation. Recognize that I am a woman. But he didn't.

Later we saw the same man in the bookstore when we were Christmas shopping and I pointed him out to Jason.

"Why are you interested in an old faggot like that?" he said.

I drive Barbara and the children to have lunch with an old school friend of hers who lives on Russian Hill. The friend looks so perfect with her jeans and T-shirt and swingy straight hair that I wonder if she has ever lived anywhere else—or at any other time. She bakes her own bread. She refinishes her own furniture—antiques that she finds in little shops. She has just painted the living room.

Children are a terrible burden, both women agree. I sit looking out the broad windows and pray that the blood from my period won't seep through the Tampax and my flowered dress onto the nubbly white sofa cushions. We have lunch on the deck and the wind blows the bean sprouts from the raw vegetable salad onto the wide wooden boards.

"You can't relax for a minute until they are away at college," the friend says. The six children play together in another room and Barbara looks relaxed for the first time since we left New York. At the head of the stairs, framed by two Ming trees in ceramic pots, there is a poster of an out-of-focus woman nursing an out-of-focus baby. LOVE SPEAKS, it proclaims. The friend gushes over Barbara's baby, who has miraculously stopped crying for the first time in days. "She's so beautiful," she coos, "sometimes I'm really tempted to have another one." Sigh. "But then I'm glad that John had the vasectomy."

At Elizabeth Arden they talk about the earthquake that has been predicted for January 14 by Madame Astra, the local astrologer. The School for Urban Studies is having an End of the World Art Show. The Trans-America pyramid may crumble, Fox Plaza may tumble, they're only made of clay, but . . . Ladies with their hair puffed out of tiny holes in plastic caps discuss their fears with ladies whose heads are wrapped in plastic bags and strips of cotton. Nervously fingering their pink smocks.

While I am waiting in an outer room of the *San Francisco Examiner* I try to make friends with the receptionist. Her lipstick is half chewed off and she wears a cheap purple dress and elastic-topped stockings that dig into her thighs when she crosses her legs. I practice my moribund reporting skills, winning her confidence, displaying my own vulnerability, prying her open like an oyster. No pearl. She tells me that she thinks it was too bad that they had to put all Californians of Japanese descent in prison camps during the war. She explains that everyone thought that Japanese troops were about to land in California. I smile and encourage her. She tells me about blackouts and evacuation routes. She says it was too bad because the Japanese are better than the Nigras. "In the Fillmore, when the Nigras moved in, the property values went right down," she says. "They didn't keep the houses up like the Japanese did when they lived there." I smile politely. I wonder how she feels about Women's Liberation.

Sometimes I'm not so friendly. Sometimes my frustrations show. I apply for a job in the Public Affairs division of IBM and they send me a ten page application form.

"Are you or have you ever been a member of the Communist party or any other organization named as subversive on the Attorney General's List?"

"I don't know," I type neatly in the appropriate blank space. "Could you send me the list?"

I call Jack Cullinan at the *San Francisco News*. I have written him three times and sent him my clips and he has been encouraging. I have met him and he is a friend of Jason's.

"Uh . . . well . . . yes . . . Salley, how are you?" he begins when I finally reach him. But I am not to be put off.

"Well . . . um . . . we are proceeding on this problem in a procedure of two stages at this point," he tells me. "Um . . . one of the jobs that we may have had . . . um . . . available required someone with extensive reporting experience . . . uh . . . and Susan Potemkin will be filling that position starting next week. The other places more emphasis on writing and . . . uh . . . rewriting, and we might be willing to consider at some point in the future . . . uh . . ." he trails off. I get the message.

I forget the anger in my heart by reading books. Long afternoons in bed. I read about FDR and Lucy Mercer and their secret drives together along the Potomac. Autumn afternoons, stolen glances. And poor Eleanor at home with his mother.

chapter 9

Evelyn is Jason's mother. I wonder about our two sets of parents. At first they brought us together, but then it seemed as if they were trying to break us apart. Then later they tried to hold us together again. Go, stop. Stop, go. Who can ever tell what parents want?

It began while I was still in Laramie; it began right after I told my parents I was coming back to live with Jason. My father called Jason and asked him to lunch at his club. My father's club is simply called The Association, and it is housed behind a gray stone façade on Forty-third Street that is said to be the last building designed by Stanford White before the tragedy. The tragedy—the moment when something clicked on in Harry Thaw's head and he went after Stanny White and shot him dead in Madison Square Garden. The scandal, oh my god, the scandal. But scandal never penetrated the musty air in the wood-paneled and

book-lined rooms of my father's club. Old men reading English newspapers in cracked leather chairs. The sagging faces
of famous scholars, lifting their drinks with liver spotted
hands. Jason was very uncomfortable. He sat in a straight-
backed chair with the name of a dear, departed member on
a brass plaque screwed to the back of it. With shaking hands
he lifted the house drink in a silver goblet engraved with the
name of another dear, departed member. Many of the present members looked to him as if they too might soon de-
part.

"What are your intentions?" my father said.

Jason trembled. For a moment he hated me. But he knew
what to say:

"I want to marry Salley."

Even after the wedding the friction between Jason and
my father persisted. On our first weekend in Connecticut
my father asked Jason if he would like to help cut some fire-
wood from a fallen oak up the hill with the chain saw. It
was an order: the trial by chain saw. My father had taken
every boyfriend I had ever brought to Connecticut out into
the woods with a chain saw. They always came back looking
miserable, and Jason did too. He was a wreck, I could see,
the minute they stepped inside the front door. He had somehow dropped the heavy machine on his glasses. The steel
chain had cracked the right lens and shattered the frame.
Without them, the skin around his eyes looked naked and
vulnerable.

"I'm never going back there," he said as we finally drove
back down the Merritt Parkway on Sunday night. "You
must never ask me to go back there."

But we did, of course, and in the end my father and Jason
shared a dozen manly experiences. They passed the football

and drove to the liquor store and split wood together and even met for lunch a few times at The Association. In fact, my parents became the parents of our marriage. The Gardens made that inevitable.

When Jason and I first visited them in Roxbury, Evelyn took me aside and confided in me. "I've known you for a long time, Salley," she said, "and I know you'll understand what I've been through." I didn't know what she meant. She had grown up in Hartford in a family with some money and a wealth of literary pretensions. In marrying Duncan she escaped their failures. He was a professor, a scholar, clearly headed for the top. Poor Evelyn. She had gambled on men, on investing her whole life in men, on living through her husband and her son. And she had lost. It was clear now that they both would have been what they were without her. Without her balanced meals and her motherly advice and her chauffering them over icy roads to the railroad station. This was driving her crazy.

On our first Christmas, her present to me was a carefully transcribed copy of a lemon meringue pie recipe written on the back of a card from the Metropolitan Museum of Art. Jason's favorite dessert. Sometimes she used a little cream of tartar to help the whites rise, she confided to me *sotto voce*, as if we were in a Christmas conspiracy to please her son.

"Oh, that old recipe," Jason said later. "Julia's is better."

But that was the last Christmas present she gave me. Something about me, or about Jason and me, annoyed Evelyn terribly, and as time passed she was less and less able to conceal it. Eventually there were bitter accusations and shouting and running out into the snow in the middle of dinner, but that was later. The first signs of trouble came through Jason's children.

"Granny says if you weren't so sloppy you would braid

our hair," Emily would say. Or "Granny says you have no right to feed us this junk." She giggled.

Once, when I was driving them back from Evelyn and Duncan's house after a weekend, they started talking about their mother.

"Mummy was so beautiful when she got married," Charlotte said.

"Which time?" I said.

"Oh, when she married Daddy," continued the innocent, the beautiful Charlotte. "Granny was showing us their wedding pictures this morning. Mummy and Daddy looked so happy together. Granny says Daddy won't ever be that happy again." She looked at me out of her pale blue eyes.

"How nice," I said.

Wedding pictures, wedding pictures, our wedding pictures had been an embarrassment. The photographer had done his job too well. There were a few portraits, but many of the pictures that we looked at on the contact sheets captured the mood of the afternoon exactly. There was Charlotte in tears clinging to her father's coat. There was Emily pushing me away from him in the reception line. There were famous writers talking with pretty girls. There I was looking lost and angry, with Jason trying to console me. In the end, we hadn't bothered having any prints made up.

"Granny says she never got any of your wedding pictures," Charlotte said. She looked up at me again and Emily looked out the window of the car. I could see that Evelyn had been complaining about me and that Charlotte had defended me. Now her open little girl's face was turned up to mine in anticipation of my perfect excuse—my explanation. She had faith that I would have one, Charlotte did, and of course I did have one, and of course I couldn't tell her what it was. Suddenly I imagined Jason's face, a little boy version of Charlotte's blondness. How many times had he looked up like that at different grownups' faces, confidently waiting for corroboration that he had been right in doubting his mother. And how many times had the answer been hidden from him?

chapter 10

In New York, most of the people we know have something to do with the literary or academic world, and most of the parties we go to are held in Upper East Side apartments with walls of bookshelves and polite doormen and large windows looking out onto Lexington or Fifth Avenue and the Park.

But in San Francisco we are invited to all kinds of places. It's a small town, and new people are a commodity. Just after Christmas everyone in Jason's department at the magazine is invited to a party for the opening of a show by the sculptor Max Angelo at the San Francisco Museum of Art. A tiny herd of Eastern sheep in our pearls and little cocktail dresses and suits, we mingle with women in long Mexican skirts with swinging straight hair and men in blue jeans and sweatshirts. The sculptures are vast angular constructions of metal and timber, some with pieces cast into twisted shapes that seem about to burst through the roof. They make me feel like a miniature.

Angelo himself is a giant, with dark curly hair and a complexion that looks as if it had been tanned about equally by whiskey and the sun. He is wearing the black velvet suit and Italian white silk shirt open at the neck that are his uniform, as I later learn from *Celebrity* Magazine. "The artist himself is important," Angelo told *Celebrity*'s Judy Brannock. "He too is part of his own work." And he moves through the crowded gallery like a king.

When I shake his hand, I notice that the first two fingers of his right hand are missing. We chat a moment; he has an atelier outside Florence (what's an atelier?), and we have spent a summer in Italy, but Jason's attempts to sound as if he knows something about Tuscany seem stuttering and silly to me. Angelo listens politely—he has a kind of knowing glance that looks as if he knows what you are about to say, but also as if he's interested in hearing you say it anyway. Then he wanders off toward a dark-haired girl wearing a long slim white dress embroidered in blue. We have arranged to have dinner with the Blacks.

On the Golden Gate Bridge a car has slipped on the cement in the rain and slid crumpling into the guardrail. Traffic has been rerouted around it and two men in uniforms and black slickers wait beside an oblong shape covered with a white sheet. We are on our way to have abalone steaks at a waterfront restaurant in Sausalito. Barbara is unhappy, I think. She is wearing a caftan to hide the weight she gained when she had the baby, but she still looks fat and puffy and her hair is dirty. She and Gerry quit smoking together about a year ago when they took a vacation on a Smokenders cruise in the Caribbean, but at dinner she takes a pack of Marlboros out of the pocket of the caftan and lights one. Over the clatter of dishes and the noise of conversation she tries to excuse herself to Gerry.

"You just shouldn't, I don't care how you feel," he says, "you just shouldn't."

Anger. The lights of the Sausalito ferry go by in the night-blue Bay outside the restaurant window. Taking someone away from here.

At the end of the winter we have a party. We have been putting it off until things got better, but it suddenly seems clear that things aren't going to get any better. Everyone comes, crowding into our white living room with the lattice-work shutters and the new houseplants and making the kind of happy buzz a good party sounds like. Michael McClure says it's the best party of the year. Even the Blacks look radiant and chat happily with strangers. I try to talk to everyone between shuttling fresh cheeses out from the kitchen and relaying orders to the bartender we hired for the night from an Italian restaurant next to the magazine office. There are old friends like Annie (who brings a boyfriend with a ponytail and an Irish Setter on a leash), and almost-strangers who have invited us to their parties during the winter, and the people from the magazine looking a little anxious as they always do these days. Even Rosencrantz is there.

Max Angelo comes late with a small-boned dark-haired girl named Amanda, instead of jewelry she is wearing a glittering Moroccan metal and enamel embossed belt. Everyone seems to know them. As the party thins out after midnight, I find myself talking to Angelo over near the window, but his air of glamour and self-assurance make me nervous.

When he asks how I am getting along in San Francisco, I tell him that I am looking for a job, and then partly out of nervousness I blurt out some of my frustration. But instead of telling me how hard it is to find a job, how there are no jobs now, he seems to understand.

"I know that it's very hard for a woman here," he says.

I retreat. "Well, I don't really know if I am gestating or vegetating," I say with a giggle. But he doesn't laugh. It's not that funny and he knows it.

We talk a little about work and he tells me that he keeps working every day even if he has no idea what he will do with the piece when it's finished. He talks to me as if I, too, were doing real, important work.

"You have to do all this to please yourself," he says. "You'll see how fickle the world is when you succeed." Something about the tone of his voice makes my success sound inevitable. And when Jason comes over to the windows to try to impress Angelo with his eager chatter about Italy and the art world I find that I am annoyed. But Max listens attentively.

"Gardens, you never cease to amaze me," he says, guiding Jason paternally toward the bar. Jason takes this as a compliment and he beams like a child.

The party turned out to be an unofficial goodbye party; ten days later, the magazine folded. It was a terrible day. Jason caught on early when he looked out his office window and saw the truck from Arnie's Liquor Store delivering cases of champagne. He suspected that Rosencrantz and Guildenstern's idea of class would be to serve champagne at a wake, and he gathered up all his expense checks and raced to the bank to cash them before the news was out.

"Guildenstern and I have tried every way we know how to keep this magazine afloat," said Rosencrantz in his unwelcome little speech at noon in the central atrium. "But we have had some bad luck and we feel at this time it is better to save what we can than to try to continue. You all know, I am sure, how much we cared for this magazine and we want to thank you for your excellent work and your faith in us. We will do everything in our power to help you re-establish your lives."

Then he declared bankruptcy.

On the last day, we stood around uncomfortably saying our anticlimactic farewells among the packing boxes. Some people were planning to stay in California and see if they could find new jobs—they had bought houses here and enrolled their children in school. Some were too numb to consider the future yet. Most of us were going back East, hoping to rebuild what we had blithely given up. It was hard not to cry. And as Jason and I crossed the Oakland bridge in the car on our way back East I remembered how the bridge had looked, a bracelet of light, the night we flew into San Francisco. I burst into tears.

It was Jason who should have cried, I suppose, but Jason never cried. Unmanly. He had lost a job, a gamble, a piece of his reputation. But for men, men of Jason's generation, there are built-in safeguards against these things. Already, even as we were driving over the bridge, the ranks of his old schoolmates, clubmates and colleagues began to form around him. There were telephone calls to friends and telephone calls to friends of friends. And by the time we rolled out of San Francisco with all our possessions piled into the car, Jason already had five promising job interviews waiting for him in New York.

At Reno, Nevada, I was driving and I had to brake hard at a stoplight. The houseplants fell off the ledge under the rear window and onto Valdi, who was sleeping in the back seat. I pulled into a parking lot and tried to repot them by the flashing lights of the quickie-wedding chapels and the all night casinos. Valdi whimpered as I brushed the dirt off him. Jason sat silently in the front, looking straight ahead, impatient to get on. Later, as we accelerated through the Nevada night, he started to talk about himself.

"I guess I should try to decide what I want for us," he said. "I guess this is an opportunity to try to figure out what

I really want to do with my life." The sandy foothills outside the car window were dimly illuminated by the April moon. We got to Winnemucca at about midnight and checked into the first open motel in a motel town. The manager was still up, propped in a grimy chair reading a mystery, a small man with a leathery face who wore a blue cowboy shirt with snaps. He leaned over the formica topped desk to tell us about the only bad check he had ever taken, as Jason wrote out a check for one room for one night. "I knew there was something funny about that guy," he kept saying, as if there was something we could do or say that would make it all right. Restore his faith in traveling men. A flyspecked calendar with a Rocky Mountain scene hung crookedly on the wall behind him.

When we got to our room with its two orange bedspreads and plastic globe lamps covered with plastic orange latticework, I started to cry again. Jason took a bottle of Librium out of the suitcase and headed for the bathroom.

"I think I'll take a sleeping pill."

"I'm going to leave you. I can't do this anymore."

"Don't leave, Salley. I can't explain why, but don't."

I took a sleeping pill too, and in the morning Jason walked out to the grocery store and brought back orange juice and corn muffins and some dog biscuits for Valdi.

It was hot. We drove ninety miles an hour. "We can just go anywhere now," I said. "We have no deadlines, no one is expecting us, we don't owe anyone anything."

This made Jason very nervous. We stopped in Elko, Nevada, for gas and the garage mechanic there convinced us that we should have the car's shock absorbers replaced.

"Look at this," he said, holding up the greasy cylinder with distaste. We wandered aimlessly around the garage. I thought about Laramie and about my life before I married Jason. Maybe I should ask him to let me off here and go back to Laramie. I sat down on the baggage, eyed by a cowboy who pulled up in a pickup truck while our car was helpless, hoisted aloft inside the cool garage. Shiny pointed boots, big hat, old Rex his German shepherd panting in the back of the pickup. All right, all right, I thought as loudly as I could. Take me. Take me up into the dry hills. I'll bake bread, bear children, rope the cattle, shine your boots, rub your cowboy cock with my big smooth white woman breasts. I love pickup trucks.

We stopped once in Iowa, on a knoll above the highway, and walked into a meadow where we could see the cars and trucks thundering by on the road below us. We had a picnic of crackers from a cellophane bag and Velveeta cheese from a little box. There were ants and Valdi dug holes in the sand and scrub. The next night we were in Ohio. Jason had said he wanted to drive all night but instead he fell asleep beside me like a child, his rumpled towhead lolling against the seat. The car hummed along on the smooth asphalt and the sparse lights of Interstate 80 flicked by in the dark. We ended up sleeping at a huge Holiday Inn perched above the road, so new that the lawns still showed the tracks of construction bulldozers. I had cramps the whole trip. Maybe from my period and maybe not. Doubled up in the front seat of the car, I would swig down Midol with the apple juice we bought at Interstate 80 gas stations and wish I were somewhere else. And hope we would never get there.

We sent postcards from each town where we slept and each gas and restaurant plaza where we stopped. "Had to skip town due to circumstances beyond our control," we wrote Max Angelo on the back of a gaudy postcard of a naked woman spread-eagled obscenely in the desert. "Wish you were here."

The job Jason finally decided to take was as a writer with the Public Relations department at Polaroid. It was a lot of money and at least he knew Polaroid wouldn't fold under him, he said. He would spend five months at Polaroid's headquarters in Boston and then come back and work in New York.

But the apartment Polaroid found for us in Cambridge was four tiny rooms at the back of a tarpaper covered building next to the vacant lot where the local children played noisy stickball all day long. It was summer. Garbage rotted in the humid heat on the broken asphalt curbs. On the walls, scraps of orange and red Marimekko fabric had been tacked up in an attempt at decoration by a previous tenant. The bed was a thin foam-rubber pad on a sheet of plywood balanced on four cinder blocks. The house next door was a shabby frame house, unpainted now, with old strips of green and gray paint peeling off one side and its door replaced by a torn Indian print bedspread unevenly nailed to the lintel. Sometimes the woman who lived there would break down and scream for hours. Bad trips.

"There goes my old lady again," her husband would say with a shrug. He sat on the stoop and drank beer. Their baby lay out in the dirt and the worn grass of the yard and there were flies on its face. Valdi panted and drooled.

In the kitchen cupboard, next to a moldy jar of brown rice, I found a dog-eared student's copy of George Eliot's *Middlemarch*. All day long I read it, huddled in the bathroom, my ears stopped with pink plastic plugs against the noise from the vacant lot. All day long I dreamed its romantic dreams. Was Ladislaw coming to save me?

At seven o'clock Jason/Casaubon would come back to the stifling apartment, old and stony and cold. Angry before he walked through the door. I could almost hear his furious inner thoughts as he came up the stairs: "I'm more than willing to listen to her but she won't even try to make things easier for me. All she does is complain. I'm taking on a new job and I need support. It's hard for me too, you know."

On the way up to Cambridge we had already started to fight. I didn't want to go. My life seemed like a Parcheesi board. Back and forth after Jason. Back and forth after Jason's jobs. (At least Jason had jobs.) At Willimantic I was crying so hard that we had to stop in a roadside rest area. Jason didn't want to stop. We had arranged to meet the owner of our new apartment and we were already late. Jason hates to be late. He was already angry. Nothing to say. We started driving again. I started crying again, tearing at his shirtsleeve, crazy with frustration, the louder I cry the less he hears me. Despair. The car swerved off the road and Jason hit me across the face with his hand. Then he stopped at last and we found a little brook down the embankment in the woods. I dabbed at my face with the cool water but the eye was black and swollen.

Sometimes I think I am going crazy. Sometimes I certainly *act* crazy; and I wouldn't be the first woman with troubles to end up . . . you know. I have this nightmare fantasy now that Jason and my parents will—all the time acting very concerned and talking a lot about my best interests— that they will have me locked up. Put away. She couldn't handle it. She just fell apart. Some nice quiet place where she can calm down and recover. And when I ask Jason if he would ever let this happen, what does he say?

"Of course not."

chapter 11

I drive down from Cambridge to Cape Cod to see Annie. She is spending the summer away from Berkeley in her parents' house in Wellfleet and wondering what to do with her life. She is Dr. Annie now. I walk along the beach at Newcomb Hollow near the water where the white sand is hardest underfoot, beaten by small surf in the shadow of the steep dunes. Joan Sinkler's old studio, the last house on the beach, rambles in gray shingles across the tops of the sandy cliffs. I was here with Annie's brother, David, once. We had escaped, in mischievous complicity, from a boring cocktail party. I was wearing a pale blue cotton dress and the wind blew it against me as we walked.

Later he came to see me again and we walked on the beach, but the promise of that afternoon was never kept. I had come back to Cape Cod from Mississippi and everything seemed strange and fat and white to me. I wore white ducks and a pale green shirt. My Mississippi sunburn—a V where my shirt had been open at the neck, and my arms and legs—looked odd and out of place in a bathing suit. Everyone else was perfectly tan. My parents had rented a house on a hill above Wellfleet Bay and the Updikes and the Breuers came for lunch the day David was there to see me. We went to the beach afterward in two cars and David and I took the Updikes' ten-year-old daughter in the back of my Volkswagen convertible. David was driving, and on the way through the woods I looked over at the little girl. She had burst into silent tears, shaking back and forth with some inner, unspeakable child sorrow.

"What is it, what is it?" I asked her, drawing her trembling blond body toward me. She buried her head in my shoulder, but her slender body still heaved with sobbing.

Years have passed since then. New homes, their shingles unfaded by the seasons, line the road down to the Hollow. Walking down the beach now, I chance to meet my own stepchildren; they are spending the summer in Wellfleet with their mother. I explain that their father isn't with me, that he is at work in Cambridge. Three young girls, we swim together, a little communion. Charlotte finds shells in the sand. She ornaments my perfectly tanned belly button with a smooth pebble. A blond stranger in a bright sari walks down the beach with a basket on her head.

"Who's that?" says Emily.

"N.O.C.D.," says Charlotte, and she smiles at a private secret.

"What does that mean?" Emily appeals to me, but Charlotte answers.

"It means 'not our class, dear,'" she says. "I heard it from Mummy, she was talking about Mrs. Simpson."

At the edge of my vision I can see Mummy. The children's mother. The monthly payments. She sits like a great sea creature, mater-familias, in one of those one-piece bathing suits gathered along the seam at the hip. I can see the sun glinting off a barrette in her brown hair. I can almost hear the arrogant lilt of her very loud voice. And I am tempted to walk a little farther down the beach. Waving a white flag, perhaps. Intrepid Salley approaches the enemy camp. Washington at Trenton. Ready to negotiate. She is threatening to sue us for more child support and private school tuition and when Jason thinks about her he yells and throws things around.

"Couldn't we talk it over like friends?" I would say. "You know you can really hurt us if you try. There's nothing to it."

"Why, of course," she would say. "I'm *so* glad you came over. I'm sure we can work it out."

The beach at night. There is bright phosphorescence in the sand. Summer magic. I scuff at it with my bare toes to make it sparkle. I complain to Annie about Cambridge and Jason. Why don't you go back to New York by yourself? she says. You could look for work and see Jason on weekends. She is impatient with me, because the problems of her empty future seem much more serious. What will she do now? Where will she go when the summer is over and the beaches are empty and the maples along the highway turn yellow and orange with the first chill? In my life, in my carefully scheduled married life, there are a hundred answers for these questions.

Jason is watching a football game on television outdoors. Our New York apartment is on the roof of an old brick building and it has a terrace surrounded by a wall that divides us from the rest of Manhattan. Over the wall, the towers and water tanks and gargoyles of the other skyscrapers are all we see of the city. It's a small two-room apartment, and on the terrace there is an electrical outlet that was once used to light the Chinese lanterns or old English streetlamps in an elegant garden that is now tarpaper and peeling brick. That's where Jason watches television when I am being difficult.

"Turn it down," I yell.

"Type," he yells back.

I can't write about New York because a thousand other writers have pummeled the city's images into clichés. The Salvation Army Bands on the corners at Christmastime. The reflections of the Fifth Avenue penthouses in the Central Park sailboat pond where I walk Valdi. Children in crisp private-school uniforms parading with their model boats. Long-legged career girls bobbing to the bus these cool, early autumn mornings, and soon, snow falling softly on the skaters at Rockefeller Center.

But I want to tell you how I feel. I don't know what I am going to do.

Jason is only here on weekends now. He will stay in Cambridge and work at Polaroid during the week until October. After a month there, and after my visit to Annie, I did come back to New York. At first I was terrified at the idea of being alone all week, but somehow the silence and the emptiness of it seemed to put me back together a little. To give me a kind of comfort that I guess I was trying to get from Jason. When he leaves on Sunday night I dance through the empty rooms in my underwear with Valdi scampering behind me. Free, I am free. I read on the bed and eat granola with my fingers. I stay up all night reading and sleep in the afternoon.

I'm sometimes even glad when Jason calls. We talk like old friends. His new job. My no job.

"Max Angelo is back in New York, did you know he has a loft in Soho?" he tells me one day. "He called me up here and I told him to give you a call and keep you out of trouble."

Jason chuckles. This is the kind of friendly patronizing remark that he makes a lot recently.

But the next day I wait for the telephone to ring and the third call, after Annie and a man who wants to sell me an Electrolux vacuum cleaner, is Max Angelo.

"I hear you're still looking for work," he says.

"Don't you have anything better to do with your ears?" I ask.

Max wants to know if I would like to go to a party at the Whitney Museum. It's the first gala opening of the fall season, he says. "It's bound to be almost incredibly boring, but afterward we can go and hear Bobby Short at the Carlyle."

It sounds glamorous enough to me. I remember the slim lion-women at Max Angelo's San Francisco opening and I wonder if I should rush out and buy a new dress.

"Don't be silly," says my friend Sara who has come over to share the excitement and help me get ready. "You'll be fine." Sara always looks just right; she is tall and elegant with short brown hair that shakes across her face in bangs. Now she goes through my closet carefully, making me try on a dozen dresses, taking a tuck here or adding a half-inch of décolleté with a pin to get an effect. Finally she decides on a long beige jersey dress that shows off my tanned back and is cut to fall open in the front, exposing the tops of my breasts. I protest mildly. I suggest a demure little gold pin.

"You're being *ridiculous!*" Sara answers. "They'll all be practically naked. Now wash your hair."

I do look terrific, I notice in the hall mirror as I leave the building, my hair straight and thick and shiny and my tanned arms and back and Sara's Elsa Peretti evening clutch. I put the ticket that came by messenger in the little lacquered box and start for the Whitney. Max Angelo hasn't offered to pick me up.

At the door, a swarm of people is pushing to get in, but the crowd parts for a moment when I flash my ticket. How will I ever find him in this mob? Downstairs around the postcard racks and over by the elevators there are knots of people, all tanned and wearing bright colors, all talking animatedly with each other about their summers, dear. In France, in Italy, even in San Francisco. *Not* in Cambridge, Massachusetts. Everyone seems to know everyone else except me. Hugging Sara's bag to my side and feeling out of place I head for the stairs to the garden level a floor below. For a moment I get a glimpse of a man I met in California, but he is deep in conversation with a girl in a lacy see-through top. Her nipples bob attentively as she talks.

I decide to brave the crowded stairs and get a drink on the garden level, and if I haven't found Max by then I will just leave. But the bar is in the far corner of the glass-enclosed garden, and as I am pushed aside by a girl in silver satin overalls I finally see Max's velvet shoulder in the other direction. I steer myself toward the shoulder, and he sees me and suddenly the knots of people break apart and he comes toward me and everything is all right.

"Thank god you've gotten here," he says. "I told you it would be boring."

We push toward the bar and without asking what I want to drink, Max orders two Chivas Regals straight up.

"Yes, Mr. Angelo," the bartender says.

Then he guides me toward the edge of the sculpture garden where one of his pieces looms gigantically against the night outside the glass.

"Good," he says, turning to me and clinking our glasses together, "now at least we can say hello."

But there is no such thing as a quiet conversation with

Max Angelo in that world. As we stand there, a stream of people come over to ask about Max's summer and to chide him about being so elusive. Christo bounds over and gives Max a hug and demands to know where he has been, and elegant Leo Castelli comes over and when Max introduces us he kisses my hand, and Calvin Tomkins comes over to say hello, looking sleek in his dinner jacket, and Robert Rauschenberg sips a Jack Daniels and assesses Max and me with brown eyes.

And really, I feel like a queen. Far away from the silly rules and regulations of everyday life. Talking and laughing with artists and celebrities as if they were old friends. These are the people who know what is really important, I think. I walk proudly along on Max's leash.

Afterward, when the party starts to thin out, we cross the street to the Carlyle Hotel.

We go through the square of light under the white and gold canopy and Max guides me a little with his hand on my arm to the left, into the Bemelman's Bar. "Let's go in here, I'd rather talk than hear music," he says.

The bar is a big dark room with banquettes and little tables and a long bar with people standing at it on the other side, and it's like stepping into a fantasy of old New York. The Bemelman's murals of whimsical dogs on their leashes and chic children skating in the park and snow falling and the sailboat pond go up the wall and over the ceiling. Max orders two more whiskies and stretches out on a banquette.

"Now," he says, looking over at me, "how was your summer?"

He sounds really interested, so I tell him about it, trying to make the month in Cambridge sound like a joke. When I get to talking about Jason's two little girls and what a problem they have always been between us, I end up telling about the way they were in the backseat of the getaway car at our wedding as if it were a funny story.

Max looks amused, but he doesn't laugh. "Why didn't Jason see what was happening to you and do something about it?" he asks.

He tells me something about his own life too, then. His two marriages and his loneliness without a wife—his fear of trying it again. He commutes between Soho and the atelier in Florence where he has some of his work cast (I still don't know what an atelier is), and a place in San Francisco. The way he says it, I can tell that "the place in San Francisco" is a woman's house, and I think of Amanda with her fine bones and big belt.

When he hails the waiter, Max notices that I am looking at his injured hand and so he tells me about that too. How, as he put the top sheet of metal in place on a piece that was going up in front of the General Services Administration Building downtown, one of the other sheets slipped and tore his hand in two. "I suppose it ought to have killed me," he says, with a shrug as if he were talking about someone else's death. "You should have heard the fantastic noise it made when it hit the sidewalk, though." A mischievous look, and then he suddenly mimics the noise of the great sheet of steel hitting concrete. "BOOOONG, BROOING, BOOOING." The heads of other drinkers turn to see where the noise is coming from and we collapse into conspiratorial giggles.

The Chivas comes again and Max ignores the decanter of water, but he doesn't seem to get drunk at all in the cross-eyed self pitying way that Jason gets drunk. And as we sit there on that banquette in the Bemelman's Bar and chatter I begin to feel a kind of lust, small pleasant electric shocks to the groin and heart. A catch in my throat. Although Max's arm is behind me along the back of the seat, he doesn't touch me, and I imagine that women always feel this way about Max Angelo.

As we walk out onto Madison Avenue together the night air is chilly. Winter is coming. I shiver and Max puts a velvet arm around me as if to warm me in a friendly way, but he looks down into my face with an expression that sends those electric shocks down to my feet and makes my face flush.

"Well, Salley," he says.

That's all. So we walk back to my apartment and sit on the sofa and drink a little Calvados and the telephone rings and I don't answer it and after that he comes over to where I am sitting and reaches down for me with his hands as if to help me up.

"I've been wanting to kiss you all night," he says.

And when he does kiss me my knees seem to buckle somehow and we go together down the hall to the bedroom. Head over heels over head and then we are in bed together and I watch him undressing in the dim light from the other room and I am waiting for him and he is next to me, kissing and sucking my breasts and then he spreads my legs with his hands and kneels between my thighs and I touch his cock with my fingers and it's long and hard and wonderful and strange and then he finds me damp and hot for him and he smiles a little and pushes himself inside me with a great moan. Oh, he says, oh. Moving back and forth inside me, locked together and flooded with that inner light. "I want you," he says, "I want to come inside you," and then he is panting and making little crying noises that I hear from very far off and we are coming together.

And then we are lying there, all of a sudden just two people again, side by side on the double bed in my apartment. I look over at him and he is smiling at me and I grin and say,

"Just another textbook fuck."

And that was when I think he began to fall for me, too.

By the next day we were both in love. Enough to say so, anyway. He had to go back to California and Jason was coming home and before he left for the airport we had lunch at P. J. Clarke's. "Every minute I'm with you it gets worse," he said. "I don't know if I can leave at all."

But I could show him how to act. Funny, I already had so much strength from Max's loving me that I was the powerful one then, cool and witty and mischievous.

"I'll call you tomorrow, I don't see how I'm going to stand it, I miss you already," he said.

"Bye," I said.

When Jason came back for the weekend that night, he asked me, "Did you have a good time with my friend Max Angelo? I told him to take care of you."

"Yes," I said. "I did."

chapter 12

"I'm sure you'll get the job," Annie's friend Peter said when he told me about an editor's position on *Critic* Magazine. "All you have to do is get along with John Peasley."

The offices of *Critic* Magazine are rent free, donated by the President of the Media Arts Society, and the beaverboard walls have been painted bright yellow.

"All of us make substantial sacrifices in order to work on something that we care deeply about," says Peasley as he shows me around. He gazes at me earnestly with soft brown eyes. He waits for my enthusiasm. He tells me about the famous media personalities I will meet when I come to work at *Critic*. He says that I will know the editors of the *New York Times* on a first-name basis. My name will become visible, he assures me. He waits for my enthusiasm.

"*Critic* will never be a sellout magazine," he says. "We get a lot of respect from well known journalists."

He takes me out to lunch and orders a Chef Salad with no

meat. He hates white bread. He wants to talk about ecology. What do I think of the great job they're doing out there in California? He has a big head with floppy brown hair, and like everyone else in the offices of *Critic* Magazine he wears jeans with a clean workshirt and an expensive-looking broad leather belt.

"Most of us don't care about the money," he says. "We're in it because we believe in it. I could make three times as much as I get on another magazine." He waits for my enthusiasm.

What can I tell him? My marriage is slipping? A series of unfortunate events have led to this curious numbness inside me, this inability to be enthusiastic at the right time, this insatiable appetite for white bread and roast beef and fair salaries and men in good suits? I seem to be floating somewhere outside the range of other people's thought and action. Out there between the shadow and the act. Unable to make myself heard, like little Emily on her birthday in Grover's Corners.

But I'm too far gone to even try to explain. Instead I tell John Peasley that I am a little tired of looking for work and that I probably need a rest. I say that I didn't notice much about the ecology movement in California. He is very polite.

"Why don't you call me when you're feeling better?" he says.

"What is this now, Friday?" I ask.

"No, it's Monday," he says.

"That's what I mean," I say, meaning nothing at all.

Actually, as I see by the calendar on the way out, it's Tuesday.

And at last I am out in the street again and it's Tuesday, a beautiful Eastern early autumn Tuesday and all I really want to do is walk up to the New York Society Library and drink in the scholarly silence of the high-ceilinged rooms and the learned dust and the open stacks. The musty smell of the books waiting to be read and read again. Years of study. And write and read, and never have to worry about if my name is visible, and never have to see John Peasley anymore.

On my way up to the library, I run into Mike Abrams in front of Georg Jensen. He is a big man, and he holds his Vuitton briefcase to his chest as he peers in at the silver jewelry.

"Hey, Mike Abrams!" I say, because I haven't seen Mike Abrams for at least ten years. We haven't spoken since he dropped by my dormitory to see me—as he had been seeing me—and I had to tell him that I was in love with Ned Winthrop and ho wouldn't be seeing me anymore. When he heard this, he took a deep breath.

"That little creep!" he said. And he walked away in the afternoon sun and I watched his back until he turned the corner. A decade has passed, but he has the same cherubic eager-to-please look on his face that kept me from taking him seriously even then. I always liked him, though. He took me to hear the Boston Symphony on his motor scooter and it was the only time that whole year that I got to wear the expensive suit my mother had sent me off to school with in the fall.

Later, when his parents gave him a Pontiac convertible, we would sit in the front seat in the dark and neck. He came from Great Neck. At first he would kiss me and then make me come by pressing his hands against the crotch of my underpants. Later, his fingers moved around their cotton edges, exploring and feeling to my moans of delight and his moans of frustration. I was in love with Ned Winthrop by then. Mike was in love with me.

Now he is a prosperous divorce lawyer with his own sailboat. "Let's have lunch," he says. We meet at an expensive restaurant near his office. I sit against a wall of mirrors at the back of the room and as he eats his steak and salad, I notice that he keeps glancing to one side or the other of my head—assessing his face in the mirrors behind me.

"You're cute as ever," he says when we part in the street afterward. "Let's not let another ten years go by."

chapter 13

I have lunch with Janie at the Harvard Club. Under the crimson canopy on Forty-fourth Street, through the backgammon room where old men shake dice in leather cups, and up to the balcony around the grill with its dark wood paneling and portraits of generous but dead alumnae glowering down at the living alumnae as they eat their steamtable liver and bacon. The Thursday special. I feel a little uncomfortable with Janie although it's something that happened weeks ago. My memories prick and bother me as we chat over our ladylike Lillets.

It was at a party downstairs at the Harvard Club and Jason and I were there and the Blacks and Janie with her latest boyfriend and I guess it began when he and I were standing by the windows outside the ladies dining room after dinner and talking. It turned out that he knew Max and that he had just been out to San Francisco and he had seen Max there. I thought of Amanda.

"I had dinner with them," he said, and then we talked a little about Max's work. Inside I churned and ached.

Them! So Max and Amanda were a *them*, then!

But I hid all that and turned with new interest to this dark-haired friend. We got along fine, of course, better than fine. I imagined Max's being told about my cleverness. "Hey, she's great!" I imagined him churning and aching, too.

So later when I went to the ladies room I gave Max's friend a little look and he followed me down the stairs. We didn't say anything but at the landing I turned around to him and he kissed me and ran his hands over the front of my evening dress and my breasts tightened and he felt them through the cloth and smiled. We went on down and went into the ladies room; it was late and the room was empty.

"Sit down," he said, and I sat on the little studio bed they have there for Harvard wives to nap on between shopping and sherry, and I helped him lift me up and pull off my pantyhose.

There was no one there but the cat.

And afterward we sat for a while completely quiet, we could just hear the faraway noise of the party upstairs as if we were underwater. And then we got up and brushed our clothes off and laughed a little. I went back to the party first and crossed the room to talk to Janie.

"Don't you think he's terrific?" she said. He came in a little later and no one even noticed that we had been gone—or that we were completely different.

"Isn't it about time we headed home?" said Jason, coming over to me. His arm possessively around my shoulders. A little drunk. Oh yes, another boring party.

Jason and I had dinner with Jason's father in the ladies dining room of the Harvard Club once. A long time ago. We were living together then, but we weren't married yet. We were just very much in love.

"I feel as if I was never really alive until I met you," Jason would say. We told each other that we had something special, that we had something other people couldn't understand, that we had something that would last forever. "You're my whole life."

That's what we said to each other.

Jason's father was disgruntled by the capacity of his only son to love. Jason's mother hadn't come into the city for dinner. I already sensed, although I never said it then, that we made her terribly uncomfortable. How could we be so happy? It wasn't fair. No, it wasn't fair.

Now we have lunch with Jason's father at the Gardens' farm in Roxbury, Connecticut. The years have not brought any of us together. The lawns are carefully trimmed but dead leaves blow across the grass. Trees are turning red and yellow and the midday sun throws beams of orange light through the bare branches of the dogwood. In the formal garden at the end of the lawn rows of pungent marigolds wait for the first killing frost. Jason's father is an old man, now. Late autumn.

I sit on a white metal garden seat in the sun and think about Max.

Jason's father stands at the head of the polished wood table to say grace over the afternoon meal: the roast, the last vegetables from the garden, the lemon meringue pie. Evelyn comes out of the kitchen with her apron on.

"*Almighty God who hast blessed the earth that it should be fruitful and bring forth whatever is needfull for the life of man, and hast commanded us to work with quietness and to eat our own bread,*" Jason's father intones, reading from the battered Gardens' family Book of Common Prayer. "*Bless the labors of the husbandman, and grant such seasonable weather that we may gather in the fruits of the earth."*

"Amen," we say, as generations of Gardens children have said before us.

Jason's father wears an old soft tweed jacket with a plaid flannel shirt and a red bandanna tied around his neck. The elder statesman, the counselor. He has known famous poets and he has advised college presidents.

After lunch the three of us walk together across the lawn, under the last elm tree on the property and past the lilac hedge as the day turns cold, and Jason's father explains that the farmer who mows the lower pasture has agreed to continue mowing it until he retires from farming in five years.

"So I guess it isn't something I'll be around to worry about," he says.

Oh Jason, Jason Gardens, what a weight, of the farm, of literary society, of students encouraged and brave hopes dashed, is laid on your narrow shoulders as this old man reaches up to put his arm around you.

Do you remember our first kisses? We were standing against the lilac hedge just over there. I had driven up to a party that your parents gave just after we met, and after dinner we walked down the driveway curving through the dark summer night and up a dirt road through those woods on the hill. We sat on the doorsill of an abandoned house up there, leaving all your past, your old parents and children behind us, trapped inside the lighted windows of the house. "You believe so much in passion that you underestimate love," Harold Nicolson complained to Vita.

I was so restless for you then. Animal Jason, happy Jason, smelling of sweet soap and the early morning. The sounds of humming and water running while you shaved. Far ago and long away. But now, whenever I look at you, you seem distracted, not listening, in another world and struggling to hold yourself together there. And I wonder sometimes if you are feeling that horrible knotting in the stomach, that rock in the guts, that is there when you know that someone you love is slowly leaving you. Eased every time they touch your arm. Eased when they smile at you, or come across a room to talk to you when there are other people they could talk to. But never really eased because you know, oh you know with a bone-chilling certainty, oh you never know anything quite so well as you know when someone you love is slowly leaving you.

But where will I go?

chapter 14

When I was a child I had terrible asthma. Heaving sobs of breath tearing through my lungs. Bronchi straining, swollen and congested with evil stuff. My father would pick me up out of the bed in the apartment where we lived on Sutton Place—when I was sick I slept in my parents' bed—and carry me into the bathroom filled with thick watery steam and for a moment I could breathe again. The sound of the shower, the painful labor of pressing the hot air down my throat. Sitting up for hours at night because it was easier to breathe sitting up, and then the pills and then slowly slumping into darkness. I missed a lot of school trapped in my own sickroom with the metallic smells of the vaporizers and soft lights and the sounds of the household going on around me. In the corner of the room there was a plump flowered wing chair and sometimes at night when I would come half awake my father or my mother would be sitting in it reading by the creamy light of the brass standing lamp, not noticing that I was awake. And then I would be flooded with warmth and happily turn over and go back to sleep.

But doctors were always an important part of my childhood. There were doctors at school and my own pediatrician and specialists and pills and shots. So that now, when I suddenly have asthma again in the sixth year of marriage, I go to a doctor.

"They'll give you an immunity shot for whatever it is," my regular doctor assures me, "and then you'll stop wheezing." I cling to the possibility that my asthma is physical.

Dr. Hoffmann's office has the air of an abandoned railroad station. There are no secretaries and no crisp sounds of typing and no voices answering the telephone. In the waiting room it looks as if a random assortment of old and poor people have wandered in off West End Avenue to rest for a moment in Hoffmann's threadbare chairs. I have come because my doctor recommended Hoffmann; his directory, I later learn, was out of date. But after my first visit with the sad and aging doctor, I haven't the heart not to go back, and I agree to come in once a week for a series of ten allergy tests.

This morning, as I wait, a slender girl with streaked blond hair and wearing a bright green slicker comes into the waiting room from the rainy street. She looks out of place, uncomfortable. She looks like the captain of the Beta field hockey team at Miss Singer's. Hoffmann bustles through the room, his gray head bowed, muttering to himself, and she tries an introduction.

"Just put out your hand and look him straight in the eye," her mother said.

But it doesn't work. "Oh yes, just a minute, oh yes," Hoffmann mumbles without shaking the hand or raising his head, and he shuffles out again. When I come out of his inner office with my sleeve rolled up, red throbbing hives beginning to form where I have been injected with cat extract and egg extract, she looks away. She has heard about this kind of doctor. She stands in the hallway shaking her head nervously at the dying houseplants and the peeling wallpaper.

"If it isn't right for you dear, just take your things and leave politely," her mother said.

"I'm sorry," she says to Hoffmann's bowed head when he re-emerges, "this isn't right for me, this just isn't right for me."

"What did she say? What did she say?" the other patients ask each other after she walks out.

"Ahhhh, she said she was afraid, she said it was too dirty, she said he was too old, too old," interprets the woman who is always sitting in the corner wearing a shabby black dress. We look at each other knowingly. The survivors. We made her feel uncomfortable. She didn't belong here.

I have terrible nightmares. I dream that Jason and I are at a ski resort. As night falls there is a last run down the mountains before the ski patrol sweeps the trails and I come off the slopes at twilight and the other skiers clump in their heavy boots up the spiral ramp to the lighted restaurant. The light is fading fast and it's beginning to get cold, the mountain brooding above me in the dark. I can't find Jason.

"I think he's already gone inside," people tell me as they snap out of their bindings and hoist their skis over their shoulders. "Come inside." But he was behind me, I know. I saw him standing at the edge of that steep pitch at the last turn above me.

Someone has been hurt.

Spotlights hit the mountain now, glinting off the snow, and pinpoint the ski patrol toboggan with its terrible load. But in the dream, it's Jason lying naked on the toboggan on a bed of cracked ice with a champagne glass of blood between his feet. I can tell that it is him at once, even from this distance, as you always recognize someone you have loved for a long time by his coloring or the fall of his hair or the little rhythms of his body. My heart sinks. Oh no. Oh no.

"Is he all right?" I call out to the patrolmen, sinister figures in black parkas, their faces masked by hats and goggles.

"No."

"Will he live?"

"Yes."

"Will he walk?"

"No."

He lies there unconscious and sickeningly, heart-stoppingly helpless. Is he ever; is he ever! A human shrimp, a human cocktail on a bed of ice. Waking next to Jason at the end of the dream, I can't erase this image of his hurtness, his innocence.

For my dreams I go to Dr. Silvertone. He is an old man with a thatch of white hair who lives and works in a once-elegant brownstone in the East Nineties. A little ivy-planted dooryard grows beneath the steps up to the big front door, and inside a comfortable room lined with old books gleams behind freshly pressed white dimity curtains that filter out the afternoon light. When I first visited Silvertone, I was enchanted by the house and the shabby street and his air of being a great old sage. Once, while I waited for him to open the heavy wooden door with its polished brass knocker, I saw two gray cats fucking in the dooryard. What I liked the best was that he seemed so unlike other psychiatrists with their sleek offices and their track lighting and their slick explanations. Later I understood that he was imitating an even more rigid teacher he had once had . . . in Vienna, before the war.

He was always very sympathetic to my complaints about Jason. "Jason may never be a whole man," he would say. "He will never be able to match your energy. You may find yourself having affairs with other men, and this would be understandable as long as they are peripheral to the marriage." Then as I left he would kiss me hard on the mouth and press his free hand against my breast.

Now he is not so sympathetic. He tells me that my idea of a woman's role in society is wrong. Worse than wrong. This desire I have to go to work is just a distraction. I can't go on living this way. Wounds from childhood insecurities fostered by my Poppa—he calls my father Poppa—keep me from knowing what is best for me. Silvertone knows. I must not quarrel with biology; the role of a woman is masochistic. The woman is the one who is penetrated by the penis, who bears the child, who must be passive, and submit, and adjust.

Silvertone was a good student, he is not obtuse, and during this little lecture he notices my skepticism, which he prefers to call arrogance. So, leaning over the edge of his desk, in front of the fading photograph of the Master, leaning over the antique inkwell, and the blue and white Canton coffee cup, and the bronze miniature of the boar from the Uffizi at Florence, leaning toward my creaky ladderback chair, he shakes a signet-ringed finger at me.

"I am not," he says angrily, "a male pig chauvinist."

As you are talking to Silvertone at the end of what he calls The Hour, the doorbell rings and he leaves, unbolting the consultation room door and going down the hall to usher the next patient into the front parlor. Then he shuts the parlor door and ushers you out through the hall. Musical chairs. But in spite of these precautions I have sometimes caught a glimpse of the person before or after me. The sad faces and awkward bodies of the confused upper-middle class, weighted down with their burdens of personal sorrows and their sixty dollars' worth of complaints against the world.

In England, where these things sometimes make more sense, people only go to psychiatrists when their wives insist on it. This happens when they are leaving their wives; when they are in love with another woman. The year Jason and I were in London, my American friend Naomi was the other woman. She was in love with Edward and he was in love with her—but he was married to Deborah. After Deborah found out about it, she insisted that they go to one of the doctors at the Tavistock clinic for therapy, but this didn't seem to make Edward love Naomi any less. She lived in an airy one-room apartment with sky blue curtains at the top of the Nash terraces on Regents Park, and Edward and Naomi would spend long afternoons on the double bed in that apartment in the sun. Head over heels over head. Naomi's stockings were always torn and her shoes were falling apart and when she opened her scuffed art portfolio to show her work old grocery slips and scrawled lists would fall out too. You know she had never done any of the things on the lists she made, but I guess Edward had had enough of lists. Naomi was energy and light and sex and beauty, and she understood the important things.

We hardly ever saw Edward that year, although he and Naomi saw each other every day. He always went home to his neat flat in Chelsea and his neat little wife in time to read his children a bedtime story.

"It's not fair to disrupt their evening schedule just because you are in love with a tart," Deborah would say. Methodically crossing some neatly entered item off some neatly written list. There were lots of photographs of Edward in Naomi's apartment, one of him dancing with her and grinning wolfishly over her shoulder. And there was a big hand-lettered sign on the door in crayon and colored ink that said EDWARD, I LOVE YOU FOREVER.

Yesterday I took a long walk with Edward and Naomi on Long Island. Her parents have a house on the dunes in Southampton and we sat on the deck in the sun. They are married now. Later we drove across the Shinnecock inlet and walked in the wildlife refuge they have there, the three of us in the late country autumn, yellow leaves and the pungent smells of the last flowers.

I asked Edward then if he always had knots in his stomach when his marriage was coming apart. I do. I told him that I thought perhaps I was expecting too much of marriage, too much of Jason. No one is really happy after all, no one even knows what that means, really. There are more important things. But Edward didn't agree with me.

"You can never expect too much," he said, and seagulls wheeled above us over the trees and flew out to sea. "There is no such thing as expecting too much."

At the end of the afternoon I drove back into New York and Jason and I went down to Soho to have dinner with his old friends the Konovers and their friend Seymour Britchky the food critic. The wine and the good meal warmed us and made us feel special and witty and Edward had given me a burst of energy too and we were all in love with each other and ourselves and the evening. After dinner we piled into the Konovers' car and headed uptown on Madison Avenue.

"Off to the prestigious Carlyle Hotel!" roared John, weaving through the midtown traffic. "I am embarking on a search for the perfect bar."

"And I," proclaimed Seymour, "I am looking for a man with no redeeming sense of social value."

"Seymour, I think you've found him at last," said John in a mock-earnest voice.

Hilarity. In the middle of laughing I looked over at Jason sitting next to me in the back seat.

He was asleep.

chapter 15

When Max is in New York City, which is not often enough for me, he stays in his loft on Howard Street in Soho near Canal Street. It's like another world down there, although it's only fifteen minutes away on the Lexington Avenue line. Up here on the Upper East Side, rooms are crowded with furniture and breakfronts and shelves of bibelots culled from grandmother's attic, and there are lots of oil paintings or modern prints on the walls above the sofas and matching chairs from Bloomingdale's fourth floor.

In Max's loft there is no furniture, only a few wooden benches made with white painted slats and built into the wall, a big double mattress on a rectangular platform on the floor in one corner, and the giant threatening shapes of his sculptures rearing up like prehistoric animals in the dusty high-ceilinged space. I can breathe there, the openness accommodates me. At Max's I am my best self. In my own apartment with my own furniture I am just a wife.

But I hate walking around Soho with Max or dropping into the Spring Street Bar or Alfredo's with him. In every block at least three people call out his name and rush over to see him and he has time for them all, a slap on the back for the men and a kiss for the women. They are mostly beautiful and dressed in the odd chicery of the world south of Houston Street, overalls tucked into soft gleaming leather boots or smock dresses belted with glittering metal or long skirts and tunics. The men give me a lecherous grin and the women look me up and down in hostile, competitive appraisal. Everyone loves Max.

In the bars where we go there is a big welcome from Gino or Joe or the other bartenders and if it's in the morning Max orders vodka and grapefruit juice and if it's in the afternoon they bring out his bottle of Chivas and put it on the bar. A crowd of groupies and friends always forms around us. I can see the anxious faces of the women in the mirror over the bottles, and Max, looking a little bemused about his own popularity, protesting at times that he would rather just be alone with me, but not leaving—sometimes not leaving until it's almost time for me to go back uptown.

You can say that I am just jealous and you would probably be right. But I never complain, at least not to Max. I never even mention that he is invariably an hour or two late for our meetings, or that he is apparently living with Amanda, or the encouragement he gives his swarms of groupies; because when I am with Max I am above all that pettiness, I am my funniest self, my extraordinary self, a woman with class, a woman who cares only for the essential things. Lateness and other women are not important. We are important. Special, with our secret knowledge of each other that no one can share.

And when we finally are alone together, making love on that double mattress in the corner of the studio and drinking

Chivas neat out of Max's glasses and laughing, I feel better than I have ever felt in my whole life.

"This is heaven," I say as we lie there and the afternoon sun comes flooding in through the high casements. And then I take a shower and get dressed and walk down Howard Street to the subway and take the Lexington Avenue line back uptown. On my way from the subway station I stop at the market and by the time Jason's key turns in the door I am Madame Perfect, changed and with the table set and beginning the cooking for dinner with a glass of white wine. Guilt is petty; I am above guilt.

When Max is away he writes long letters scrawled in his huge handwriting on heavy vellum pages with his Rapidograph pen. The mail sometimes comes before Jason has left for work and so we have arranged it that Max writes my letters in care of my friend Sara. During the morning, if she is walking by my building, she puts his letter in my box in the lobby and then later when I have had time to read it and daydream a little she calls me up.

"What's the bastard up to now?" she says. And sometimes I go over to the apartment where she lives with her boyfriend, Jim, and we gossip and drink tea and another day is wasted on Max.

He is away more than not, in Florence supervising the casting of a piece, or in San Francisco, but I keep the thought of him in a secret interior place in my mind and retreat to it often. He loves me! It's a still, small island of self-esteem and contentment. And when I see posters of Max's work or hear him talked about, or when Jason brings home articles proclaiming him the greatest sculptor of the decade, I feel enhanced and powerful. I comfort myself with this thought: If such a man can love me, I must be more than just a housewife.

chapter 16

In New York City, if you have a car and you keep it on the street instead of paying hundreds of dollars a month to put it in a garage, you have to repark it two or three times a week. Each street has parking prohibited from eight to eleven in the morning Tuesday and Friday on one side of the street, and from eight to eleven Monday and Thursday on the other side. Work it out. This way, there is always one side of the street that is theoretically empty between eight and eleven on the mornings when the city sanitation trucks come to flush out the gutters with their hoses and brushes. Except Wednesdays and weekends. Water sluices down past the curbs with old newspapers and little dog turds and garbage bobbing along in the current like the make-believe boats in *A Child's Garden of Verses*. A frigate under full sail runs down the wind toward the grating at the end of the block.

What people do here in order to get a parking space is to

move their cars at ten in the morning, parking in one of the spaces prohibited from eight to eleven of that day. Then they sit in the car for an hour until the space is legal, or until they think there is no more chance of a meter maid or a cop coming along. They won't ticket a car if there is someone sitting in the driver's seat, even if it is parked illegally. That's big city courtesy.

So what happens is, during the hour of parking, everyone comes at about the same time from the space he or she has parked in earlier in the week and we all shuttle our cars back and forth so that the maximum number of fellow parkers can get into each block.

Jason goes to work, and I park the car. But many of the parkers on my block are men. There are the daring types who risk getting a ticket and leave soon after ten, giving the rest of us defiant looks, and there are the cautious ones who stay until eleven and who, if you give them half a chance, will tell you horror stories about cars' being towed away at ten fifty-five and wrecked forever by the tow trucks and their owners' never collecting any insurance because they were parked illegally.

To pass the time while they wait in their cars, some people read the morning newspaper, some do accounts or crossword puzzles or balance their checkbooks. I usually read a novel.

This morning, just as I had gotten to the place where George Emerson kisses Lucy Honeychurch among the violets on that hill above Florence in *A Room with a View* (neither of them realize that Charlotte Bartlett is watching), I heard someone playing scales on a trumpet. I looked up from the book and saw that the man sitting in the car parked in front of me, a late-1960s Ford Fairlane coupe, was practicing on the trumpet to wile away the hour. The brass of the instrument flashed in the sun. When he saw me looking at him, the player adjusted the rear view mirror in his car so that he could look back at me and play at the same time. And then he started to serenade me with a long, sad sonorous tune. It was the kind of tune that Benny Goodman used to play on the clarinet when he was a kid and everyone gave him a hard time.

"Benny, don't be that way," they would say.

And he used to just go and sit in the twilight on the roof of the building where he lived with his family and play this long, lamenting sort of tune. Later, when he was successful and had lots of money and no one gave him a hard time anymore, he called that same tune "Benny, Don't Be That Way."

In the *Village Voice* I read a story about how marriage is really just a form of prostitution. I am very suggestible. I think that maybe I stay with Jason because he supports me. I remember, when I first met him, how impressed I was by the fact that he had his own trust fund; I realize how much I now wish it were more substantial. It's hard to be tactful about having someone depend on you for money, I suppose. Especially now that we all think that money is power. Mendicants are no longer saintly men. If you are supporting another person financially, how can you justify it? How can you feel, and how can you make them feel, that their presence alone is worth money to you? Especially if you have no children, or if they are grown. It can't be that you are paying for their body in bed, or their housekeeping abilities, or their charm and class, because none of these things are for sale. Only a whore sells her body, only a cleaning lady sells her housekeeping abilities, only a geisha sells her charm; and a wife is none of these things.

How can it work anyway, this money business between men and women? Why do some people pay for other people if not in return for services rendered? Charity is no longer saintly either. Is marriage just another exercise in acquisition, with markdowns on older models and racks of possible purchases displayed to their best advantage? Is courtship just another hype? You've got me.

And so has Jason for that matter. Really, I tell myself in the depths of this funk, I don't have much of a choice anyway. I can find someone else to support me. I can shut up and cook. I can go on trying to find a job that will enable me to support myself. I can't leave Jason when you start to think about it. I'm trapped. Once I had a job, once I actually did support myself, but that was years ago and now I can't. Jason has to. Jason hates to talk about things like this.

I dream that I am in a meatpacking factory. There is a long tunnel in the dream with trains roaring through it and a chute for blood and a chute for entrails. The sound of death. The smell of slaughter. I am a lady journalist writing an article for *Travel & Leisure* magazine about meatpacking factories. Henrietta Peck. I am shown into a dimly lit room where eight of the packing plant's workers are waiting for me to interview them. Standing against the wall, they are all gorillas, ex-convicts, rapists and murderers, men who have taken this worst of all possible jobs in the final stages of desperation. To them I can see that I am just an object, an object of contempt and scorn and their grubby lust.

"Hey, lady!" one of them yells over the din of the machinery, but I can't tell which one.

I look fearfully across the room toward the glass doors where the worst stage of the slaughtering is done. Where animals shit their hearts out with fear before the mallet falls on their soft heads. And one of the men sees my fear and begins to laugh derisively. The one on the right, with the dark hair and a stubble of beard. And then I see that they are all laughing. . . .

chapter 17

On Saturday morning Jason and I have what passes for a
friendly talk. I urge him to admit, and he admits, and I
admit that we are miles apart, that we are both turned off,
and that something should be done about this state of
affairs. This orderly life we are leading, this not fighting, this
carefully scheduled peace and quiet is just a sad truce.
That's what I say, and Jason agrees, although I think for a
moment that maybe he was happy with the sad truce. We
go uptown to PB 84 and look for furniture with the other
nesting couples; matching Burberrys, matching Guccis. I
buy a dress at Saks and bring it home for Jason's approval.
He approves. We read much of the night and go south in
the winter.

On Saturday we usually have people for dinner or go out
to a party, and this Saturday we are invited to a big evening
at the poet Ruth Wallach's penthouse apartment. The rooms
are crowded with eccentric characters perched on the Louis

Quinze couches and around the piano and on the steps out to the garden. Familiar-looking models and messenger boys, the cook from Ruth's favorite Chinese takeout place and last year's Pulitzer Prize winner for history. There is a man called André wearing jodhpurs and a hacking jacket and carrying a riding crop. And an Italian painter with smoldering eyes who has a studio on the West Side where he spends long afternoons in bed with women who are interested in art. Ruth says he fucks a lot better than he paints.

A red-faced drunk in a plaid blazer with a Westchester Golf Tournament patch on the pocket—his clubs are probably in the hall—tells me that he spent last Christmas in the island stockade at Dutch Guinea.

"I've served my time," he slurs, weaving across the room. There is a buffet being served in the dining room and toward the end of the evening, after the Pulitzer Prize winner and his chic wife have left, I notice another drunk, a woman with long dark hair wearing cheap slacks and sunglasses although it is almost midnight. On the make: I see her approach the Italian painter as he stands in the doorway, she leans on the doorframe to steady herself.

"My name is Joe," she pleads.

He walks away. She gets the same treatment from the man called André and a little later I see across the room that even the golfer has given her the brushoff. Jason and I are sitting on the floor behind the sofa talking to Alex Harmon and Lucy Beanes when suddenly this dark woman, who has settled herself uneasily on a chair near us, heaves her body across the space and drapes herself over Jason, who is sitting next to me. I cringe.

"Oooohhh," she coos to Jason, "you are so wonderful, I can tell you are the most wonderful man." At first Jason is embarrassed, I guess, but he has had a lot to drink too, and not many people telling him how wonderful he is lately, and slowly he begins to respond to these drooling endearments. He doesn't get up or disentangle himself or push her away. His arms are around her and he whispers comfortingly in her ear.

"That's a nice name," I hear him saying. "I think that's a very nice name."

A lot of people are watching by now, the scene has become the center of a dying party, and the men who had already pushed her away look on with little sneers.

"You can tell that he's kind of flattered," says Alex Harmon; and when the drunk falls asleep, snoring softly with her dark head in Jason's lap, I get up to go.

When we get home, Jason pretends that he can't understand why I am angry. Maybe he's not pretending.

"It was nothing," he says. "It was just an accident, for Christ's sake, it wasn't my fault that she fell over on me. What was I supposed to do, be brutal to a guest of Ruth's?"

"If you want to make out with other women, can't you do it in private?"

"Don't be ridiculous, I don't even know her name. You're making a big deal out of nothing," and Jason stumbles self-righteously into the living room.

"I'll sleep on the sofa tonight," he says.

But he lies down and passes out fully dressed and later I come in and undress him and half carry him to bed.

The next day we go for a long Sunday walk with Valdi across Central Park through the Sheep Meadow. Jason is very hung over and repentant and I am forgiving. His head aches. We talk about our marriage in earnest voices. Jason says we should act as if we were going to stay together.

He does not say that we are going to stay together.

We have dinner at Clarke's and walk home and go to bed early. We're both tired, of course, but I still want to talk. I want something from Jason. Something more.

He starts to fall asleep.

I ask him not to fall asleep.

His eyes begin to shut. He opens them with a start and studies his fingernails.

I ask him not to fall asleep.

Suddenly he sits bolt upright, looking at me from a thousand miles away. He is angry.

"I don't think this kind of inquisition is going to help us," he says. It gets worse. Soon we are out of bed, really fighting again, and Jason is standing against the wall and screaming at me to leave him alone.

"You're out to get me, you're after me," he yells. "Get off my back, get off my back." Later I lie in bed, crying while Jason sleeps. Sometimes I feel like never getting out of bed again.

But I am afraid to leave Jason. How can I do it? I spend hours adding and subtracting from my savings passbook to find out what I already knew. I need someone to support me. Also, I am afraid to be alone, although this is the last thing I would ever admit. To spend Saturday nights by myself with a bottle of whiskey in front of the television set. Reruns of *Wuthering Heights*. Weekends in New York with nothing to do. A woman without a man. Friday night in the supermarket shopping for food for one. And I am afraid, too, to shatter a marriage. *What God has joined together.* I loved Jason enough for that. I loved him enough for anything, I thought. I still love him.

Sometimes, in the late afternoon from wherever he is, the studio in San Francisco or even from Florence (an atelier is just a studio, it turns out), Max will call.

"I love you," he will say. "I love you, Salley, I don't know what to do with you except love you."

And talking to Max I am suddenly witty, suddenly tough, suddenly above the silly little doubts and angers that assail

me in everyday life. It works the other way too. Sometimes
now in a fight with Jason when I'm at my self-pitying worst,
crying or yelling at him or huddled up on the sofa sobbing
and feeling sorry for myself, sometimes then this other Salley, Max's friend Salley, seems to be watching me in amaze-
ment.

"Who is this drip?" she says. "If she is so unhappy, why
doesn't she get off her ass and do something about it?"

When I am with Max, when I have been with Max, I am
magnificent. Truly superb, with that disregard for the petty
and the self-pitying that characterizes God's favorite
people. I can do anything. Max loves this in me, and I love
myself for it too. Sometimes I even wonder if that is what I
am really like. But I'm too smart for that. And I'm afraid
that if it were Max I was married to and living with and
sharing American Express bills and angry phone calls from
ex-wives with, that I would be the same way with Max.
Eventually. Sometimes Max talks about marriage, he wants
to get married again and have some children, and once I
tried to explain to him what marriage meant to me, why I
wouldn't want it. Why he wouldn't. But he didn't understand at all.

"I'm not like Jason," he said, laughing down at me from
one of the ladders in the studio where he had gone to fix a
crossbeam. "It wouldn't be like being married to Jason,
dummy." And he shook a handful of plaster on my head and
we both laughed.

Still, I think the situation worried Max. He talked about it
again and again and eventually he probably would have
convinced me, but it turned out that Max needed a woman
who was much surer about marriage even than he was.
Years later, when I was staying at the American Academy in
Rome, I met Max's first wife at a cocktail party in the Villa
Aurelia, and in that foreign setting with the orange twilight

closing in over the Janiculum we talked about Max. Because he is the kind of person everyone talks about.

She told me that when she had been seeing him for about a year and he first mentioned marriage she seized on it.

"Good idea," she said, "let's go tell my parents tonight." And by the time Max started to waffle it was too late. Plans were under way. She was so sure, and that made him sure enough. And they got married.

But here, in New York with Jason, Max's voice on the telephone and the certainty of his love seem very distant. Once I got a whiff of his real distance, too. Max the hedonist. I had called the studio in San Francisco at night, desperate to talk to Max, to get a love fix, and one of the assistants whom I didn't know answered the phone.

"Is Max there?" I asked.

"No."

"Do you know where I could reach him? This is a good friend."

"Well, I'm not sure, but after six he is usually over at Amanda's. Do you have that number?"

When Jason came home—he had been working late that night—I was suddenly swept off my feet by a rush of love for him. What a kind man, I thought, what a handsome man, what a rock. I made a late supper and we drank white wine and afterward we ended up for the first time in weeks in each other's arms in bed.

"I love you," Jason said. "I know we are in trouble but we'll get through it. I keep forgetting how much I love you."

And I thought, this is my home. This is where I belong.

I have an appointment with Red Beaumont at *Newsweek*, but before I am shown into his office I wait in an outer hall next to the elevators.

"Mr. Beaumont's secretary will be with you in just a minute," the receptionist says.

People come and go through the hall as I wait and there is a slim dark woman with a fluffy cloud of salt-and-pepper hair talking to a man with a briefcase in front of the elevators. She is wearing a tweed skirt and a silk shirt and she has an air of authority that he seems to respect. So they have women here, I think, encouraged. But Red Beaumont is a gentleman of the old school, a solid man in a Brooks suit who peruses my resumé over Benjamin Franklin half glasses.

"I can't understand why you haven't gotten a job already," he says.

Mutual, sir.

Out of the corner of my eye I can see a construction of Max's on the cover of a glossy art magazine on Red Beaumont's coffee table.

"A good possibility," Red Beaumont wrote in a memo about me after I left. (I found this out much later.) "She came across as a pleasant, with-it sort of person in an interview. She might be worth a try."

"Everyone wants to work in a place like this," he told me then. "I'm on your side, but it may take a while. Why don't you write me again in a month or so?"

chapter 18

One Saturday evening we go to a dinner party at the Blacks'. They came back from San Francisco about a month after we did, and their new apartment is furnished to look as if they haven't been away for decades. There are humpbacked Victorian sofas and hunting prints and Gerry's grandfather's grandfather clock and even a *tableau morte* of stuffed birds under a glass dome. It's the kind of party we go to often. We know everyone and feel comfortable with them and we all suspect one another of being second-rate. There is one New York celebrity (a film critic), two pretty girls, one English publisher on a New York scouting junket, the Albrights, the Wallaces, Barbara Black's cousin Harry Rosenthal (a writer who lives in the Village), and an aging woman who is principally known as the mistress of a famous man. She wears a black sweater and a heavy Alexander Calder silver pendant; the famous man is not there.

Crossing the room at midnight I notice that Jason has gotten terribly drunk. He is talking to Harry Rosenthal and propping himself up against the wall, but when he leans away from it he can hardly stand up, and when he goes to get our coats, which are stacked on the bed in the master bedroom, he caroms off the walls of the hall.

Harry gives me a knowing and unpleasantly lecherous look.

"It happens a lot, doesn't it?" he says.

I am furious, mortified and angry that Jason should give a second-rater like Harry Rosenthal that kind of opportunity. The literary world is not benevolent and I see in Harry's mocking eyes his own sense of advantage, and his intention of dining out on the story of Jason's drinking. Stupid fucker.

We leave the party and start downtown. Walking, if you could call it that. I hold Jason at each curb, guide him across each street. He is not at all appreciative. He demands to be let go and strikes out self-righteously on his own, only to trip over his feet and come swaying to another halt. He is a tall man and people stare. He slumps against a lamp post with a ticking box bolted to its side.

"I'm just waiting for this noise to finish," he says. He sees that I am angry through his haze and begins to drunkenly berate me for my low opinion of him. He tells me that I don't understand him.

"I'll show you," he says, pointing a wavering finger more or less in my direction. "Some people listen to me, some people respect me even if you don't. Harry Rosenthal respects me."

I am angry. "Would you like to know what Harry Rosenthal said about you?" I ask.

"Hunh?"

So I tell him what Harry said, getting his sarcastic tone into it, too, and it hits Jason like an electric shock. He starts to sob, standing there on Park Avenue.

"You've destroyed me," he sobs, "you've destroyed me. I hope you're satisfied."

He starts quickly off in the other direction, suddenly sober. I go too, and grab the sleeves of his overcoat. He pulls himself out of the coat and starts running crookedly but fast up the sidewalk. (Jason ran the 100 in 1.5 at Yale.) The coat is in a heap on the pavement. I pick it up and follow him, but he is already way ahead. We cross Park and go down Seventy-seventh Street by the hospital. I think I can see him at the end of the block but it's dark and there are other people on the street. I begin to run too, weighed down by Jason's coat. I trot up Lexington and across a block where I think I see him again and then down Seventy-eighth toward Third Avenue. I get a glimpse of his tweed jacket under a streetlight way ahead of me for a second, but it isn't him and I have lost him. He's gone. I put the overcoat on over my sheepskin coat and go home. In the elevator, Raymond the night man gives me a funny look.

"I see you are all bundled up," he says.

Jason doesn't come home. I lie awake. In the morning I call the hospital, the Nineteenth Precinct Police Station and the Chelsea Hotel. No Jason. I wait alone, feeling that I shouldn't call anyone, that the disappearance of a husband is a disgrace not to be shared with friends. He has no keys, no coat, no money. Where can he have gone? I think about suicide—he was headed for the East River—and then I decide not to think about it.

In the afternoon, I leave the keys with the doorman and take a long walk downtown to calm myself. It is Sunday, a cool gray day, and I walk down toward the empty streets around St. Patrick's Cathedral. A light drizzle begins to fall. When I get back, Jason has just come home.

He is desperate and repentant. "How could I treat you that way?" he says, holding me so tightly that it hurts. "I didn't realize how much I need you. I thought I could live without you and now I know that I can't." He spent the night asleep on a bench in Grand Central, wandering around hung over and glassy-eyed until they opened the drugstore, then he shaved with a disposable razor he bought with the change in his pants pockets. A melancholy man. Now he can't hug me enough.

"Oh God," he says, "it's over and I'm back and I love you. I'll never leave you alone again."

Now who can quarrel with that sort of talk?

About a week later the overcoat was stolen. Jason left it on a coat rack in a restaurant where everyone else had left their coats and when he came back after lunch it was gone.

Like me.

On weekends we always seem to fight. I can never remember how they start, but the fights always end at the same impasse. Why can't he listen to me, I want to know. Why can't he believe that I am on his side? Why can't I be a partner in the marriage? And he wants to know why I am always after him, why I won't leave him alone.

"Get off my back," he says.

Naomi calls from London to ask if we would like to go skiing with them at Chamonix. Would I? Suddenly I think that maybe if we could go, ski together, swinging in wide curves through fresh powder, stopping at a stand of trees to grin at each other in the cold air, skis parallel, edges dug in, flexing the knees and pushing off, carving and swooping across the hill away from each other and toward each other, throwing up plumes of snow in perfect rhythm chased by the oncoming night, open fires, four-poster beds; maybe if we could ski together it might be all right again.

"I can't," says Jason.

Instead we go to Washington, D.C., and stay at the Hay Adams, a favorite of Jason's.

Like us, the hotel has seen better days. Our windows look out on an airshaft. It is gray, wet weather and freezing cold. The ponderous government buildings we walk past on Connecticut Avenue are vast and unfeeling and empty. We stroll across the wet grass of Lafayette Park toward the White House and a small squirrel comes up to me and touches my hand with a cool nose.

And we make love between the pale yellow sheets. But even this ends in a fight. In the morning I wake up first and order blueberry pancakes and coffee and we eat and chatter away happily at each other with blue-stained teeth. But then I want to make love again, and Jason wants to leave. He is afraid we will miss checkout time. Jason hates to miss checkout time. He tells me that I am selfish and irresponsible and trying to humiliate him. I tell him that what he is really afraid of is life.

So it goes.

We check out and wander in our sulk through the grim streets. I make an elaborate show of watching the time so that we won't miss the train. Jason always worries about missing the train. But we have already missed the boat.

Isn't it strange? People fall in love with each other all the time. You see them often, holding hands, or giving a fond nuzzle on street corners or country roads. There was no reason why Jason and I had to fight so much. There was really no reason why we weren't in love. But I often think we even daydreamed about murdering each other. Bringing the number-10 cast-iron frying pan down on his cold, self-righteous face. Strangling me. Why is this simple thing that everyone can do—loving each other—why is this simple thing so difficult?

Tomorrow morning I will go with Jason to see Dr. Silvertone. Everyone will be very polite. Jason and I are very polite to each other. We each loudly profess concern for the other's welfare and the other's future. We even act affectionate. He wakes me up by pawing my shoulder and pretending to be a giant cat. I buy him fish, fresh fish for his dinner. He brings home a bottle of wine. At night, I curl up next to him in bed.

But something is missing here. Inside me it feels as if something has been turned off. I can't accept the idea that this is all there is for me, that this is marriage, that this is it. *It.* I can't accept it because I'm turned off and I'm turned off because I can't accept it. If Jason could go back to wooing me, listening to me, loving me, perhaps I could turn on again. But he can't, because he is turned off. We don't even fight anymore.

I call Mike Abrams at his office. We have had lunch together twice since I met him on Madison Avenue last fall. Now, he has a cold. He flew in to New York last night on the Red Eye from Los Angeles and he was kept awake by the Nottinghamshire rugby team singing dirty songs about Hitler in their cockney accents. Or at least, that is what he has decided to tell people, and he has to tell me about it before I can say what's on my mind.

"Salley," he says when it's finally clear to him. "I hope you know what you're doing."

"How much can I get?" I say.

"I just don't want you to get hurt, Salley," he says. "Probably about a hundred dollars a week."

So when Jason comes home I tell him that I think we should try living apart for a while. It seems to me, I say, that I still love him but we are making each other miserable. He looks miserable. He agrees. We'll probably get back together, I tell him, we just need a rest. We'll certainly stay friends. There's no rush.

And this is the way a marriage ends. We sit across from each other in a green windowless conference room in the offices of Benjamin, Beller, Jacobs and Quinn, each flanked by a lawyer. My lawyer, recommended by Mike Abrams, is a short man with a flat, expressionless face. In private, he calls Jason's lawyer "shitburger." In private, Jason's lawyer calls my lawyer "the Jew." Staying friends is not what they have in mind. This conference table was not designed for amicable settlements, with its computers and its piles of documents and endless coffee brought in by secretaries. My client this and my client that. Silent moments. We stare at the wall, we stare at the green baize table surface, we stare at each other's lawyers. Please sign here.

More than a year ago, when things were at their worst in San Francisco and Jason and I had already started fighting, he brought home one evening, to that white-latticed apartment, a little box wrapped in brown paper. A present. And in the box was an ivory netsuke of two gorillas, a big one and a smaller one like us, both with very sulky little faces but with their shoulders pushed firmly together against the world. I don't like you sometimes, but I need you a lot.

This morning I noticed that the little gorillas had somehow fallen off the bureau in the bedroom, and when I picked them up off the floor I saw that the big one's foot had broken off. It upset me so much. More than the lawyers or the divorce or being alone or putting asunder what God had joined together or anything else. I felt awful. I guess I am more sentimental about things than I am about people really, although I like to say that I don't care about possessions. Objects are so defenseless, so completely helpless, it's worse when they get hurt. People bounce back. I'll sleep with a stranger to get revenge on Max, I'll cheat on my honest husband, I'll curse my aging parents because they don't understand my divorce, and that's all in the game. But when an ivory gorilla given to me long ago by a man I supposedly don't care about anymore breaks its stupid toes off, I can't stop crying.

chapter 19

Éze village is one of those medieval hill towns on the Riviera that has over the years become a haven for English speaking painters and writers, and more recently for English speaking groupies. It began with F. Scott Fitzgerald, who used his friend Sam Barlow's house in Éze as a model for Dick and Nicole Diver's house in *Tender Is the Night*. Then about twenty years ago, after the war, one of the larger villas perched on the steep rocks above the Mediterranean was bought by the Famous Poet, an aging giant with gargantuan appetites who still sometimes hikes down the narrow cliff path to the beach on summer afternoons to eye the local talent from under his broad brimmed hat.

Since then, English and Americans have flocked to the place, some to work in a friendly atmosphere where the wine is cheap, and some to play. They crowd the beaches at the foot of the cliffs with their polyester swimsuits and bright totes, chattering in the cafés, driving up the prices, and giving the little village a gloss of money and an air of disenchantment that separates it from the other towns along the Corniche.

I remember seeing Jennifer once, before I knew her, in the upper market where the local villagers shop. Lady Jennifer Moulting. She was asking about the vegetables in that odd French the upper-class English have—perfect grammar and vocabulary spoken in an entirely English accent—as if they couldn't be bothered to pronounce the words in that ridiculous way the French do.

"Avez-vous des aubergines?" she was saying.

She always reminded me of Maud Gonne with her tallness and her big dark eyes and cloud of red hair, so different from her two-year-old daughter's pale blondness. The little girl's name was Angel. And Patrick, Lord Patrick had the air of a British Consul to a nonexistent country, reticent deep blue eyes in a tan face and a lean body under fine cotton lawn shirts from Turnbull and Asser and white linen pants, and the espadrilles we all wore.

I developed a terrific crush on them both—I "fancied" them as Patrick would have put it—and I got to know them well. When I went to the beach alone, leaving Jason inside the cool rooms and tile floors of our house, and saw Patrick lying on the sand, my heart jumped up.

Later someone told us, someone took it upon themselves to tell us as people always do, about the Moultings' terrible past. "Oh, I've seen you with them, and I thought you should know about their past," they said.

Jennifer had tried to kill herself once, and instead through a grim mistake she had failed in suicide but killed her two children. Five and six they were. Out on the kitchen floor with the oven going. She had asked the woman next door to take the children for the afternoon, but the woman next door was busy. And now they're dead.

"I was pretty well drunk for a whole year about ten years ago," Patrick told me once. "I guess you know I had reason to be." Jennifer in the hospital. The children dead. Finding them there like that and not knowing how to carry on with life afterward. Two dead children and a fine crazy wife.

But these things were never talked about among the four of us. Instead we went to stay at their house in Portland Place, in a tiny guestroom at the back. There was blue-patterned wallpaper and an ivory handled mirror on the dresser and a perfect little brass bed. There were signs, though. Signs of death's quick visit. Once, taking the dining room tablecloth off for the laundress, I saw the drawings of a child older than Angel etched into the tabletop. Initials: P.M. And in books sometimes I would come upon the scrawls and drawings of children and the tentative beginnings of script. It was strange to see those ancient marks; Angel cooed and smiled on the couch. But the strangeness was only part of it. I stayed friends with the Moultings, closer in a way than I have been with anyone else. Partly because so much was always left unsaid between us . . . and this is the stuff that love is made of. Partly because my heart was caught by their human endurance, their doing the only thing they could do, really, even though it was unthinkable. How could they go on after that? They just did.

chapter 20

When you think about people like the Moultings, divorce seems a little anticlimactic. It hardly counts in the great sweep of human suffering and experience. Everyone gets over it. Especially when there are no children.

Nevertheless, it hurts.

Nothing to do, nowhere to go, and worst of all no one to blame it on.

In this sudden vacuum, my reaction was to create rules and schedules more rigid than anything I would have tolerated while I was married. I didn't want to be one of those dazed men or women you sometimes see, wandering out at dusk for their breakfast while the rest of the world whistles home from work. Valdi helped a lot. Two walks and two feedings to wrap the day around, and my mornings began in Central Park with him trotting past the sailboat pond and smiling at the nannies with their charges in playsuits and polished navy-blue baby carriages.

But Valdi was also a *memento mori*. When Jason and I bought him in London, agreeing to postpone our first child awhile, we were very happy. I would wake up in our little flat on Kensington Church Street to Jason in the bedroom chair trying to feed that wriggling brown puppy's body his vitamin pills. Vivaldi, we named him, because he was so sprightly, so perky, so gay. And in the afternoons we would walk him in Hyde Park and sit on the penny chairs near the Serpentine while he tore around on the grass.

Now, at six o'clock when Jason used to come home, Valdi sits at the door waiting. Sometimes the elevator door will open and he will hear it and wag his pointed tail against the wooden floor, but of course it's never Jason and he settles back down with a big doggie sigh and an odd glance over at me. When it's Valdi's dinnertime he carries his rubber bone into the bedroom, wagging his tail, and then he runs down the hall to the kitchen with it—one end in his mouth and the other bumping on the floor to make it squeak. That's his trick. No, I haven't let him up on the bed. But our day ends after the eleven o'clock news when he curls up on the rug under my desk, gives me one last quizzical look and drops off.

I have lunch with Annie at Clarke's. Spinach salad. She tells me about her new job at Columbia, but what she really wants to talk about is David. She wonders if he will ever get married, she wonders if he will ever find a girl. Something about the way she says it makes me realize that she is in love with him, her own brother. Annie and David.

"What does he need with a woman?" I ask her, testing this hypothesis. The responsibility! The difficulties! The late-night phone calls! The mess!

"I don't think he wants to fall in love, he's too smart for that," I say innocently. "And anyway he has you."

Annie beams at me. "Let's have dessert," she says.

I tell her that I have seen David teeter on the brink of falling in love and then, at the last minute, hold back. I do not tell her that it was with me.

All my friendships seem to have come off their moorings, adrift. Annie was always my counselor, and now I am becoming hers. My parents are acting like children, sulking and silent. But the most enormous changes are with men.

"I'm married," I used to say, or I would work a reference to Jason into the conversation. And that would be it.

Max isn't around either.

"For Christ's sake, Salley, if I had known you were going to do this I would have arranged to be there," he says on the phone when I tell him that Jason is gone. Instead, Max's summer schedule is all booked up. In June and July he has promised to teach at a new American school for young artists that some friends are starting in Florence, and in August and September he has to be in San Francisco to install his big show, which opens in October.

"I'll try to get there, little Sal," he says. "Don't be blue."

But I know he won't. Max is a little nervous about what he will find out about me when I am free, I think. He loves the simple, tough, sexy sneaking-downtown-for-stolen-afternoons Salley, not the lonesome complicated creature who has nightmares and talks to her dog. Maybe he doesn't want to hear about a marriage that wasn't his, either. That's what he means when he says:

"I don't know what to do with you except fuck you and love you."

chapter 21

I go to the Chase Manhattan Bank to change our joint account to a single account and to put my savings in it. The bank is a temple to money, with high ceilings and vaulted windows and tellers behind their marble altars. At the stone balustrade at one end of the nave I am ushered across a green carpet to a seat next to a bank officer's desk. He is about forty, with a broad face and short graying hair.

"I know you're upset, but I'm sure this was the best thing for both of us, Mother," he is saying into the telephone in an exasperated tone of voice. "Sometimes marriages just don't work out. Okay? I'll call you later, okay?"

"I take it you're getting divorced," I say. Instant empathy. A sign on his desk reads Vice President John A. Anson.

"Call me Jack," he says. And by the time we have spent half an hour filling out bank forms, my name, my father's name, my mother's maiden name, we are on friendly terms. Two tough singles in the big bad city. "Look, could I take you out to lunch sometime?" he says as I get up to leave. We have lunch at Clarke's and he leans across the table over his bacon-cheeseburger in the dim light to confide the details of his divorce. Happy families are all alike, wrote Leo Tolstoy. So are New York divorces.

He thinks his wife may be seeing another man. He wonders if he is still in love with her. He has been living with a temporarily unemployed actress in her studio apartment; she's a terrific girl but he is about to move into his own place in a brownstone off Central Park West.

The next time we have lunch we meet at Bloomingdale's, where he has been shopping for furniture and a new sweater. Summer is here and sweaters are on sale. We go across the street to Daly's Dandelion and, leaning over a chef's salad this time, he reveals the latest installment. He has broken up with the actress.

"She was really hurt," he says, giving me a soulful look, k-chomp, k-chomp, k-chomp, k-chomp, "but I knew I could never be in love with her." I can't tell if he is implying that he could be in love with me. It's Saturday afternoon and the sun warms us when we step out onto Third Avenue.

"Why don't we walk across the Park and I'll show you my new pad," he says, trying to make this careful plan sound spontaneous. He smiles at me; there is a piece of lettuce caught in his front teeth. "I think I'll head back uptown," I say. "I'm expecting someone for a drink." (The little mare was standing there calmly in the stall but then just as I almost had the door shut behind her she bolted and pushed it open and me over with it and galloped out onto the grass, free, wheeling in the sun.)

"Okay," he says. "I'll call you."

The summer evening settles down over Central Park. I walk Valdi. We go in at Seventy-second Street and turn onto the grassy hill, and when I let him off the leash he races in circles of freedom around me. We walk down to the sailboat pond and as we pass the boathouse a man comes bouncing out of the men's room on the south side. He is black with his hair slicked down in a side part and a red bandanna around his head and in the steamy summer heat he is wearing a blue duffle coat, worn out at the edges with two toggles broken. I lean down and pick up Valdi and we get off the path to try to avoid him, but he starts prancing around us in circles, the laces on his worn-out shoes flapping in time as he chants.

"I washed my face, I washed my hands, I washed my feet, I washed my legs, you have to be clean for these things."

I ignore him, walking stonily on, and he prances past, stopping a prim secretary on her way home from work to tell her about his new cleanliness.

"I washed my face, I washed my hands . . ."

The next day I have a ladies' lunch with Catherine Cutler at the Women's Exchange. She is an old girlfriend of Jason's from before I knew him, and when I first met her her icy beauty terrified me. I could never be like that. Now I give her a pep talk. She is looking for a job in journalism. I tell her to consider each person she writes to lucky to hear from her. I tell her to stop worrying about inconveniencing people. I tell her to drop names. I tell her to badger the bastards. I tell her they are all about to be sued for sex discrimination under the new Equal Opportunity laws and they would be lucky to get her. I tell her she is too good to be a researcher. I forget to eat my chicken salad and when I get home I have a terrible headache.

At Radcliffe, when I was a freshman, there was a girl in our class named Amy with a thin face and a cloud of frizzy black hair. She always seemed much older than the rest of us. At the time—it was before I met Ned—I was trying to be friends with a group of students who were starting a new college literary magazine. It never got off the ground, but there were a lot of parties. At Bill's apartment in an old frame house on Hammond Street. At Jeffrey's. I was in love with Bill. Once, in a car, on the way to a poetry lecture in Boston, he put his arm around me to get something out of a side pocket and left it there on my shoulders. He took me to a Chinese restaurant on Brattle Street and confided in me— he was still in love with a girl who had broken up with him that summer. Pamela. Pamela, she hurt him terribly.

"Perhaps someone could open that door for me again," he said. Long looks over the fortune cookies. My heart pounded. I didn't know what to say, and whatever I should have said, I didn't. Later Jeffrey took me to the Chinese restaurant and walked me back to the dormitory. We sat on the flagstone steps. Nothing happened. Mike Abrams was the first man I ever really kissed.

But Amy fucked all those guys. Once we were demonstrating against Civil Defense at a bomb shelter that had been put up for propaganda on a plot of city grass in downtown Boston. Big liberal deal. We carried signs and we were on the front page of the *Boston Globe*. The shelter was open for visitors, two cramped rooms, one lined with canned foods from the I.G.A. market, the other with two bunk beds, and while we demonstrated Jeffrey and Amy went inside and fucked on the narrow bed meant for the last survivors of Armageddon. I saw them come out smirking. The newspaper didn't mention it. Fuck the demonstration, fuck the bomb, fuck it.

Now Amy is in New York, she lives in a studio in Westbeth under the West Side Highway and she is trying to sell her paintings. They are patterns of splattered color and sometimes the splatters spill over onto her clothes and hands.

After lunch I usually lie in bed and read, and one afternoon just as *Daniel Deronda* is losing my sympathy by falling for the prim goody-goody Miriam instead of regal and troublesome Gwendolyn, the telephone rings. It's Bob O'Brien, a friend of Jason's who worked with him for a while on the magazine. When Bob was divorced about a year ago, Jason and I "helped talk him through it," as he said. This meant hearing every detail of the breakup about ten times. How Jane told him to get out. How Jane and his mother always hated each other. How he wasn't sure if Jane could live alone. How he thought maybe he should have been tougher with Jane. How he was worried about the golden retriever he had left with her. How much he missed her sometimes.

Now, Bob wants to know if I would like to have dinner with him on Saturday night.

"I know what it's like," he says.

He takes me to a Mexican restaurant in the West Sixties, and during dinner he keeps filling my glass with raw white Mexican wine. Three bottles. My head swims. Over dinner he confides the details of his divorce, talking in an emotional *sotto voce*, as if they had always been too painful to discuss until now. How Jane told him to get out. How Jane and his mother always hated each other. How he thought he should have been tougher with her. How he was worried about the dog. "You must be having some of the same feelings," he says mournfully, edging his hand toward mine across the table.

"No," I say. "I got the dog."

On Tuesday night I invite him to my apartment for a

drink. Well, he took me out to dinner. He escorted me home in a taxi and kissed me on the cheek at the door. Now he bounds in with a bottle of Mexican wine and a big bunch of peonies. He looks more relaxed in jeans and a polo shirt, almost attractive with his tan and blue eyes and high forehead. I put the flowers in a vase, an old wedding present. We have a glass of wine and talk about his divorce. What should he do about Jane?

Every time he gets up to pour another glass of wine, he moves a chair closer to me until finally we are sitting knee to knee on the couch. "You look fantastic, sitting there like that," he says. I stare at my feet in sandals. I go out and lean against the wall of the terrace. It's twilight and the lights of the city are turning on around me. Bob follows me and leans next to me against the terrace wall.

"You're a very lovely woman, Salley," he says.

"I know," I say.

"Now don't be afraid," he persists, turning my stiff body toward him by the shoulders. "You don't have to be defensive with me. I know what it's like. It's very very scary the first time you feel something for another man." When he kisses me his teeth grate against mine, and he draws back to give me a proprietary, self-satisfied smile. Cat and canary. I notice that his hair is thinning and that he has carefully combed it over the top of his head to hide the balding patch.

"I know a good Mexican restaurant near here," I say.

I know all the tricks of the trade,
I know just how the maiden is made . . .

. . . the chorus of the Hasty Pudding song the year I was a junior. And then Eddie Bailey, rigged out in an ill-fitting pink flapper's dress with stockings falling down around his hairy legs, would reel out onstage in a slapstick imitation of a tipsy woman, look around, and confide to the audience in his suddenly very masculine voice.

"Do you know how to make a pot of coffee? Welllll," (rolling his eyes) "well, first you tell it that you love it!" Howls of laughter. Eddie shrieked offstage trailing his costume-department feather boa.

The only trouble was that Eddie Bailey told my friend Peggy that he loved her one day when they were sitting in the yard of Dunster House, and she believed him. He was the captain of the football team that year. And that summer, in the Bailey family sailboat about a mile off Oak Bluffs, he headed into the wind and took her in his arms and she let him do everything to her. On the floorboards of the sloop, with the sails flapping in the wind and her sailing shorts pulled down in the sun. But next fall when we all came back to Cambridge, Eddie ditched her for the prettiest girl in the freshman class. And Peggy was so mad she decided to go and pee on the place where Eddie had told her that he loved her. She did, too. We went one night and I stood guard. I don't know if she felt any better afterward.

The editor that I have an appointment with at the offices of the *Village Voice* is a slight, wise-cracking character named Joel Stansky whom I have met a few times at parties with Jason. He leans back in the folding chair in his tiny office—a poster proclaiming IMPERIALISM SUCKS dominates one wall—and peruses my resumé and clips.

"I'm not sure what we can do for you right now, Salley," he says, "but let's go have a drink anyway." We go uptown to the bar of the Regency Hotel, the only place in New York that serves Harp Irish beer, Joel explains, and we sit on red leather barstools among the plush and mirrors. A slender man with wild-looking hair in a tweed jacket and a pleasant looking girl in a little two-piece dress from Saks. The bar is empty when we go in at around four o'clock, but as we sit there it fills up with businessmen having their jolt of whiskey at the end of the day and worn-out lady shoppers drinking cocktails. Joel and I gossip about the magazine world and people we know and he doesn't bring up Jason. I know that he was divorced about a year ago, and he doesn't bring that up either. Instead, we laugh a lot. I always liked him. And after awhile we are alone together, the only two funny smart people in the world of assholes and dopes. We take a cab up to my apartment and instead of dropping me off, he asks if I would like to have dinner. We walk Valdi in the cool evening, the trees in the park making green canopies under the streetlights. Summer night.

When we get back to my apartment I go into the kitchen and open a bottle of white wine. When I come out to the living room, Joel is carefully measuring out five narrow lines of white powder from an elaborate antique snuffbox onto a piece of glass.

I watch him quickly inhale three lines of the powder through a brand new ten-dollar bill rolled up like a straw, and then, when he hands me the bill, I inhale the remaining two. "There aren't many girls I would want to turn on with," he says, carefully measuring more of the powder into lines. "Here," he picks up a few stray grains, "rub this against your gums." And we sit there rubbing the powder into our gums and he pours a glass of wine.

I feel very much in his power, but very wary at the same time. There is a pleasant buzzing sensation in my brain as if a mild electrical current had been plugged into my nervous system. I feel relaxed, but wide awake.

We drink the white wine and talk some more and forget about dinner. Suddenly it's two in the morning. We are sitting opposite each other in the armchairs with the empty

wine bottle between us talking about astrology. Joel stops
and looks at me intently.

"My problem is that I'm sitting here wanting to seduce
you," he says, looking away now, out the window at the
night. "I don't usually feel this way."

"Is that it?" I tease.

"But I don't think it's a good idea," he says, getting up
from the chair and staring down at me. "It's too close to
your being with Jason, and I would probably fall in love with
you. That's the last thing you need right now." He pockets
the snuffbox and heads for the door.

"I'll call you tomorrow," he says.

I stand up, too. Suddenly, I don't want him to go. I think
that I will be lonely if he goes. "We could just do it and not
think about that stuff," I say, "I mean we could just do it to
satisfy ourselves physically." That stops him, he leans
against the kitchen wall.

"I've done that," I say.

"I've done that," he says, taking off his tweed jacket.

You know, sometimes men don't seem to mean what they
say at all. There's all this sweet stuff before they get it in
there, all this I-don't-usually-feel-this-way and I'll-probably-
fall-in-love-with-you and it's-going-to-mess-up-this-or-that-
long-term-relationship-for-me. But afterward it turns out
that it's still a scalp for them and a surrender for you. Like
always.

In the morning I walk Valdi and read the *New York
Times* while Joel sleeps. He looks grungy and hung over,
snoring away in my bed with his clothes thrown over the
chair. I wake him up with a cup of fresh coffee, but he
seems disoriented and confused. I wait while he showers
and dresses, and when he finally wanders into the living
room I am sitting on the sofa, reading.

"This refrigerator is ridiculous," he says, peering into my

empty icebox. "Why don't you have any beer?" And then he gives me a kiss and he's gone. "I'll call you tomorrow if I can," he says as the elevator door shuts behind him.

I dream that I am standing on a high ledge above the freight tracks at Croton-Harmon Station and somehow I know that the train is coming and then I see that Valdi is standing next to the tracks with his dumb rubber bone in his mouth, looking around for me.

"Valdi, Valdi, come here," I call. I whistle. But of course (because this is a nightmare) he can't hear me and then the train comes and he disappears behind it and my heart sinks. There could never be another dog like Valdi. But as I watch, the train passes and there he is, brown body rolled over and over and covered with dust but still moving, trying to get up on his little feet, the bone thrown clear of the tracks. As he picks himself up, I call out again.

"Valdi, Valdi," and I start down toward him. But of course he doesn't hear me and just then some workmen come along the track, which is now (itself) in a very high place at the edge of a cliff and the workmen pick Valdi up and look around. I wave and scream frantically, but of course they can't hear me, although I can tell they are looking around to see if anyone owns this little injured dog. Valdi is dazed and his head sort of swings and the man who is holding him gives up, I guess, and shrugs his shoulders because who wants a hurt stray dog, and throws him over the cliff. His body falling over and over and out of sight. There could never be another dog like Valdi.

chapter 22

Sometimes it seemed as if everyone in New York knew Colin Willes. Thriller writer and socialite. The author of the best-selling mystery *The Caper Caper*. Even I had met him a few times at publishing parties with Jason, and so when we passed each other on Madison Avenue three weeks ago, we stopped to say hello. I was wearing my number one jeans and a gauzy pale blue shirt and I looked great.

"Aren't you Salley Gardens?" he asked.

And, remembering who he was and because he is attractive and I wanted him to know I said, "Well, not exactly, but I used to be."

We had a cup of coffee at the Skyline. He is living in the Hotel Adams and has just finished another book, but he seems poised at any moment to take off again, for another country or for more research. Cool Colin.

"I'll call you Monday, and perhaps I will be able to persuade you to have dinner with me somewhere," he says.

On Monday I am not at home, but on Tuesday the telephone rings late in the afternoon.

"Is Mrs. Gardens there?" he asks.

"You can call me Salley," I say, but he doesn't laugh.

"I wonder if you would like to foregather this evening?" he says.

"I thought people only foregathered in Henry James novels."

And so it went.

Colin always seemed intent on being so impeccably correct that no one could possibly take exception to his behavior—no matter what he did. He did, too. Each one of his books, as I noticed when I made a special trip to the library to look them over, was dedicated to a different woman. Pale blue eyes, a craggy, sophisticated looking sort of face, clothes a combination of worn out English tweeds and the best of Brooks Brothers.

He picks me up at the apartment and admires the view from the terrace. I dig out an ancient bottle of cassis to make him a kir.

"I'm in a linen tablecloth sort of mood," he says. "Do you think you could stand La Goulue?"

"Your usual table, Mr. Willes?" says the headwaiter.

But Colin isn't quite what he appears to be, either. "Who do you think is smarter, you or me?" he asks over our steak and pommes frites. Soft banquettes, light gleaming out through the cut glass on fresh flowers. The Ladoucette chilling in a silver bucket. He never drinks red wine.

Later in my apartment I go into the kitchen to open a bottle of Johnny Walker Red and make a drink and Colin follows me in. He opens the cupboard and picks out two glasses. He gently takes the bottle out of my hands.

"Let's go drink this in bed," he says.

Even in the morning his façade is intact. He is up, making

fresh coffee, feeding Valdi scraps and singing snatches of Puccini when I open my eyes.

"You're making me feel pretty vulnerable," I complain.

"Well, a lot of women think I am a shit," he says. He smells of Jason's shaving lotion.

"A man who says he is a shit," I tell him, "is a man who was late for lunch once and still feels guilty about it."

He likes that. I win a mildly affectionate look.

"I have to go down to Washington this afternoon," he says, "but I'll call you when I get back on Thursday."

"Oh, Colin," says Catherine Cutler. "I never really understood him. I guess it was my fault." Her blond hair is dirty and she is wearing sunglasses and too much perfume. She hasn't found a job yet.

"Actually I even thought we were engaged once." She looks upset. We are having lunch again. "I flew over to Rome to marry him, I thought, but when I got there he had booked a separate room for me at the Hassler. I hardly ever saw him and after about a week I came home."

"If it's Colin Willes you have your eye on now," says Mike Abrams, "you can just forget about it."

"I've known him for a long time," Joan tells me on the phone after we spend a tedious half hour discussing her current love affair with the lead guitarist in the Chocolate Banana. "I never really felt that I *really* knew him if you know what I mean." She giggles. "He's so, sort of weightless. I don't even know who he is seeing or anything. Wasn't he involved with Catherine Cutler for a while?"

"Well I've seen him around, but I don't know him too well," says Max in his biweekly phone call from Florence. "I get the impression he's homosexual. Why, did you run into him at a party or something?"

Colin calls on Thursday.

"I wonder if you would like," he says in a soft, precise voice, "I wonder if you would like to go to a small party at my agent's house, which is in your neighborhood, and then perhaps we could have dinner and go to a movie."

It's a beautifully orchestrated evening. A real date. An hour at the cocktail party where Colin makes sure that I always have someone interesting to talk to. Very solicitous. Very *galantuomo*. A funny French movie at the Sixty-eighth Street Playhouse, and then a late supper at the Carlyle.

It was always like that, perfectly planned and perfectly pleasant. Even the sex was like that. Gently undressing me and making love and then if I hadn't come he would slide his head down between my thighs until my whole body answered to the expert flicking of his tongue. We never talked about ourselves, but once or twice he said things that seemed to me to mean that I was something special for him.

"I'm ready to slow down," he said one night. We were having daiquiris at The Sign of the Dove and the summer evening blew against the cream lace curtains. "I've had enough of just appreciating women. I want to have someone to feel responsible to." And he patted my shoulder.

But after that, he didn't call for a week. Two mornings on my way to the Park with Valdi I saw him in the distance. A tall form striding down Madison past Parke-Bernet. But it was too far to call out to him or catch up without looking a little desperate. That's what the whole thing was like, too, in a way. Glimpses of Colin in the distance, glimpses of what it could be like, and then he would vanish around the corner.

"I'm terribly sorry," he would say later. "You should have called to me. We could have had a nice lunch."

When he did see me, we had a wonderful time. "I had a wonderful time," I would tell him. But in the interim he would hold himself back, disappear, letting me feel his withdrawal and lose my balance. I always wanted just a little more of Colin Willes than I got. As a result, in spite of Max, and in spite of the fact that I have read *The Red and the Black* three times and should know a little something about the fickle heart—as a result, I sort of fell in love with a man that I knew hardly anything about. Except I knew that it would be a silly mistake to fall in love with him.

So it became a kind of contest. An unofficial and completely unacknowledged competition to see which of us was the toughest, the coolest, the hardest to get. (He was, but there were times when he didn't know that.) "Who is smarter, you or me?" he asked me again and again: once as he left the apartment in the morning, me wrapped in a towel; once over our whiskies at the King Cole Bar in the St. Regis. And that became the most important question.

There is a certain kind of man, usually one who has been brought up by women, who always holds himself back. He counts his personal value as finite. He thinks that his essential self is a precious substance or something, and that if he gives it away, if he lets it go, there will be less of him afterward. Women are thieves; that's what his mother told him.

Men like this would rather be alone anyway, I suppose. What else can it mean that they only want women they can't have? Their lives are always carefully scheduled, there are charts and there are calendars. It's all a mistake, though. The more you risk, the more you reap. The more you give, the more you get.

I know that now.

One day when I am visiting Colin at the Adams, I see an

invitation lying between the monogrammed silver brushes on his bureau, and I notice out loud that I have also been invited to the same party.

"Would you like to go together?" Colin asks. "I thought I would skip it."

"No," I say, "I sort of thought I would skip it too."

But in the end, I go. Colin hasn't called for a week and Max's visit on his way from Italy to California is at least ten days off, so I wash my hair and put on a long summer dress and walk the ten blocks through the warm evening to the party apartment. I'm still a little nervous about going to parties alone, now, but I am also excited.

It's a pleasant party with a big bar and dancing and lots of people I know. I start talking with some old friends and Peter gets me a drink and we are standing in the corner catching up with each other when I see Colin, summer blue blazer with brass buttons, crossing the doorway in the other room.

"Oh," I say, "there's Colin Willes." My stomach sinks.

"Yeah," says Peter, "I didn't even know he was back in New York. He certainly hasn't lost his touch, you should see the dish he came with! She's over there by the window."

I look. She's gorgeous. My stomach oozes out through my feet onto the floor. I smile woodenly. Peter introduces me to a bald man who has his own vineyard in Rockland County. I try to sound interested. I especially try to look interested. Pinot Chardonay. Phylloxera. The harvest. Out of the corner of my eye I see that Colin has noticed me and that he is circling closer to the conversation and then standing politely at my shoulder until I have finished discussing the growing of grapes.

I turn to him with what I hope is a smile and he's just grinning.

"Hi, stranger," he says. "I don't suppose I could persuade you to dance with me."

So we dance, and I try harder than I have ever tried to do anything before to keep him from knowing. I laugh. I twirl. I do not ask where he has been. I do not ask who he is with. I do not ask why he hasn't called me. Cool Salley. But after one dance I leave the party and I guess that gives me away anyway.

"You should have emptied the punchbowl on his head," says my friend Sara.

chapter 23

I meet Max at Kennedy airport in the afternoon. Picking my way through the crowds to find his broad, beaming face. I congratulate myself on not having gotten too involved with Colin Willes. That might have been awkward. Still, I feel distant and a little nervous about seeing Max, and he is always the last person off the plane, as if he couldn't be bothered. But then the minute he comes down the ramp with that big smile, looking like I am the best thing he's ever seen, everything is all right again.

And for a few days it was better than all right. Golden days. Wine-and-pâté-and-crusty-bread-at-midnight-eaten-together-in-bed days. Walking-the-streets-at-four-in-the-morning-and-laughing-together days. Making-love-and-holding-each-other-and-talking-until-dawn-comes-over-the-roofs-of-the-summer-city days. And then we pulled the curtains and fell into a deep short sleep. I always slept like a child next to Max.

"I love you, Salley," Max would say, making a little song out of it, "let's get married, oh let's, oh let's!"

And when I tried to explain why I didn't want to, not right away anyway, it sounded too serious to be serious and it always ended up in pillow fights and tickling and hiding each other's underwear. We washed each other's hair in beer and gave Valdi a bath in it too.

"I want to have children," Max would sing, hopping around the apartment in a little dance, "I want to have your children. I want children and dachshunds too."

"Greedy," I would laugh back. "Greedy, greedy Max."

He was greedy, too, for sex and food and drink and my responsive flesh. I had never made love that way before. Kissing the stumps of his fingers and loving his wounded hand because the accident hadn't killed him and then kissing his arm and then each other and then his mouth and his cock in my mouth and at the edge of the bed or anywhere he could catch me and we came again and again and fell asleep and woke up together. Head over heels over head, as if it could never end.

Then on Wednesday, Max announced that he had to go downtown and work at the loft and he was gone all day and he came uptown exhausted, his fingernails caked with plaster, and smelling of cheap cigars. I had been expecting him all day and missing him so keenly it was hard for me to believe that he was there. He hardly was and then he went back to the loft to work.

"I'll see you in the morning," he said. But on Thursday he didn't call until about six and then it was to tell me that we were driving up the Hudson to a suburban restaurant to have dinner with an old teacher of his.

"I want to see Tom Logan," he said. "He's a wreck now but he taught me a lot about welding once."

He used to be a great teacher, but now he's a great drunk. We stood at the bar of the restaurant. Tom Logan had been drinking all day. Spittle slid down the creases on either side of his mouth.

"I have a bad tooth," he said.

Max poured Logan's drink into a larger glass so that he wouldn't spill it. The liquid sloshed back and forth.

"I know how to do this," said Max, "I've had a lot of experience drinking on ships."

We laughed. I admired Max's form, his generosity toward a man who had helped him once. Across the restaurant dining room I saw some people I knew. Dan Singleton and his wife and their daughter and her new husband. The daughter is about my age and we were friends as children.

I remember her first wedding. It was perfect, Jason and I agreed. She was beautiful, ethereal, slender and swanlike. Her husband was pleasant and rosy-cheeked and very, very rich. The ceremony was in the garden of the Singletons' house, informal but correct. Clearly right. Women in picture hats and pastel dresses from Saks and men in summer suits. As we sat around the linen covered tables drinking Moët et Chandon and eating wedding cake from Dumas the couple wandered away from the party and sat under a tree on the grass where we could see them. She in a long lacy white dress with the sunlight weaving in her hair. He on the grass at her feet. Later she threw her bouquet and garter at the crowd from a stone wall above the garden. Her younger sister caught the bouquet. Her husband hesitated just a second before taking the garter off her slim thigh, a WASP grin at the guests, just the right amount of gentlemanly lust. And off they went in the limousine, leaving us with our fantasies. They were going somewhere wonderful. The marriage lasted about a year.

And here she was. Max, I'd like you to meet Wendy Singleton. Wendy, Max Angelo. Tense under her blusher. Hair skinned back. The new husband silent. I had the feeling the four of them had come here to discuss something important that none of them had the nerve to bring up.

Max and I drove back to New York, and the next morning we woke up together and had breakfast at the Skyline. And just as I was about to suggest, with a giggle, that it was about time we went back to bed, he decided that he should go downtown and work some more. "I've got to finish this piece tonight," he said. "There's no reason for you to come down. Why don't you have an evening to yourself and we'll have all day together tomorrow?" Even a little misunderstanding like this with Max turns me inside out. There is so much at stake.

So when I got back to the apartment, alone, just to take my mind off it I decided to call Colin. Just a distraction. And what could be safer, I certainly know that I am not in love with Colin now. He sounded pleased to hear from me. We talked for a while and he told me that he was going to Ireland for a few months on Monday to do some research for a new book and said he would love to see me before he went. Could I have dinner?

Of course.

And after dinner Colin and I went to hear Bobby Short's second show. It was a lovely evening. Colin had ordered ahead at the restaurant and gotten the best table, and I was so relieved to be away from the turmoil of Max and his why-won't-I-marry-him and his work that I felt this tremendous fondness and gratitude toward Colin.

We sat in the dark bar at the Carlyle and drank Ladoucette and held hands and talked gently and quietly to each other and Bobby Short played "As Time Goes By."

> *It's still the same old story*
> *A fight for love and glory*
> *A case of do or die . . .*
> *The sentimental things apply . . .*

"SAM, SAM, I thought I told you never to play that song again!" and Humphrey Bogart bursts through the door of Rick's Café heading for the piano.

"But, Mr. Rick . . ." and Sam shrugs his shoulders and then Bogart sees her sitting next to the piano and he stops in mid-stride because he never got over loving her, war or no war.

Then, sitting on the banquette and looking over at me at just the right moment, Colin asked me to go to Ireland with him. A tender question.

"Why don't you come with me?" he said. "You could do some writing and you might do worse than me. You know you can say no to things all your life, but sometimes you have to turn around and say yes." He gave me a little kiss.

It was like some wonderful fantasy. The lights. The music. Some role for Bogart and Bergman. Because by this time I knew that Colin didn't mean these things, and he knew that I knew. Two lovers in a darkened café, white wine, holding hands, and this delicate and loving conversation. The sentimental things apply. . . .

But that isn't what love is. Even Bogart knew that, at the end of the movie. Love is waiting all day for Max to call and feeling sick inside all the time because your guts are tied up in knots and being insanely jealous of a woman you have hardly met who is three thousand miles away and being raw with pain because you are not together and then ecstatic because he is here but desperate at the same time because you know he will go away soon and your whole life will be shattered and you'll feel more alone than ever.

I know that now.

chapter 24

A gray Saturday morning. I walk Valdi and the earth has
the smell of early spring. It's the first cool day in this steamy
August. After lunch I go to pick up some books at the library and because I see it on the librarian's desk, I take out
Edith Wharton's *The House of Mirth*. Cool Mrs. Wharton
for these hot, hot nights. I cruise through the supermarket
on my way home—tunafish, dog food, shampoo—balance my
new checkbook and settle down with the August issue of
Cosmopolitan. Goodness, what would Mrs. Wharton have
thought of this magazine? How to develop a friendship with
your skin. What to say when your man finds out that you
have been having an affair with his boss. How to do almost
anything with patterned sheets.

Max is gone. He leaves an awful emptiness that Valdi and
I rattle around in. The apartment seems much too big for us.
Without knowing it, I guess, I was counting on his visit for
something and it protected me from the loss of Colin and

even a little from the loss of Jason, so that now it's a triple loss. He called early this morning. It was about four, I guess —it was dark and I couldn't see the clock face. He seemed very upset and he was in a bar somewhere and other people kept grabbing the telephone away from him and introducing themselves.

"I think we should have a talk," he kept saying. "I think we should have a talk." I wasn't even sure what he meant, I was still half asleep, but it sounded as if he is in pain, too.

"If we ever get over each other, Salley," he said, "we'll both be so cool and rotten that nothing will ever touch us again."

My friend Elizabeth has been here this week. We met each other at Éze the summer Jason and I spent there and since then she has lost a man she really loved, and Jason and I have lost each other. It seems like a long time ago that the four of us were together, swimming and hiking over the ancient terraces there, going up to the café in the evening or driving down to Nice for a concert. Now she lives in Rome and when we see each other, about once a year, we don't ever talk about our losses and we never really know when we'll see each other again. I can't afford to go to Italy, certainly, and her visits to New York depend on the business trips of the man she is living with now. We don't write.

Yesterday, which was the day she left, we took a walk together in Central Park; she was carrying a straw basket with two handles and we each took one. Like the summer couples walking to the beach at Éze. People stared. We giggled. In front of the gorilla cage in the zoo a school field trip of black kids downtown from Harlem for the day were watching the antics of the new baby gorilla. Patty Cake. The little gorilla swung from her tire and clambered up the bars and after each acrobatic feat she performed one of the kids would say, "I can do that, I can do that."

Elizabeth and I sat on a wooden bench opposite the Pierre Hotel and waited until we felt up to saying goodbye. So far away, doesn't anybody stay in one place anymore? But in the end, instead of saying goodbye she suddenly said to me,

"I am all right now, don't you think I am all right now?"

"Of course you're all right, you're fantastic," I said.

But we both knew what she meant as she waved and kissed me and walked across Fifth Avenue.

I am not all right now.

I call Jason—about once every two weeks we have a friendly little conversation—and this time I ask him if he ever gets depressed. He tells me that he was very depressed for a while (he makes it sound as if his depressions are worse than anyone else's), but then he went to see *The Three Musketeers* and that made him feel better.

"Why don't you go and see *The Three Musketeers?*" he says.

Shanny Stevens comes to take me out to lunch. Some mutual friends have suggested that he call me. He is young and has curly black hair. He wears an expensive white linen jacket that's very rumpled and Gucci loafers with one bit missing. He sits on the sofa in my apartment and sips his kir and when he gets up I notice that the back of his creamy white jacket is covered with Valdi's short tenacious brown hairs. Little fellow sleeps on the sofa sometimes, I guess. Heh, heh. We have lunch at Clarke's. I don't tell Shanny that he is covered with dachshund hairs. He tells me how difficult it is to see a lot of women at the same time. We commiserate. You can never remember whom you have told what to. You forget who you saw which movie with.

"You have beautiful hair," he says. "I like so many girls in New York, but now I have met you."

He tilts his horn-rimmed glasses up on his head and gives me a long look out of his green eyes. I think I am supposed to suggest that we go back to my apartment. As he walks away down Lexington Avenue the last I see of him are the hairy brown patches on the back of his jacket.

At night I sit and read Mrs. Wharton, naked in front of the laboring air conditioner, trying to stay cool. Valdi pants on the floor. Lily Bart and Lawrence Selden are having tea in his apartment. He is an indigent bachelor and she is a beautiful woman who needs to marry money.

Suddenly I am assailed by the smell of skunk. Here, twelve floors above the New York City streets with the lights of other skyscrapers twinkling over the terrace wall. Has one come up in the elevator? I get up and put on a T-shirt and shorts but there is nothing in the hall. Even Valdi smells it and gets up and snuffles around trying to figure it out, but neither of us can find one anywhere.

These days, Mike Abrams spends his free time working on his sailboat, *Dreamstuff*, which he keeps at the Yacht Club on Long Island Sound, and he often smells of varnish and fiberglass and the fittings of the sails. He is good to hug, and safe. Tonight I went down to his apartment with a bag of groceries and cooked dinner for him. Poached salmon and hollandaise. Dill and cucumber salad. Apple tart. I wasn't married to Jason for nothing. I had a wonderful time cooking, it seemed like years since I had made a whole dinner. I set the table and brought everything in to Mike, playing geisha. But I know he would like it better if I was feisty and attacked him and gave him a hard time. That's what he always loved me for anyway. Why do all men want to be told that they are full of shit? Can't they figure that out for themselves?

One of the two elm trees at the foot of the orchard below my parents' house in Connecticut has been slowly dying for years, and last week my father and Don Hayer, his neighbor from down the road, decided to fell it themselves. They greased the chain saw and went to work about five feet up the trunk on the north side of the tree. The old elm fell neatly, crashing down onto the mint patch next to the driveway with some of its branches resting in the brook that runs through the property. My father and Mr. Hayer started cutting the tree away from the stump, but as Mr. Hayer worked on the underpinning branches, the tree suddenly came free of the stump and rolled over onto my father, knocking him to the grass and pinning his legs. Blood poured across his face, but he was silent. The neighbor and the gardener from the house next door had to lift the tree off him. My mother was in the house calling the doctor, but of course once he was free my father refused to go to the hospital. "It's just a flesh wound," he said. So now he has a swollen eye and ten stitches in his forehead.

"What an incredibly WASP accident," Mike Abrams said. "That could only have happened to your father."

I wake up in the night, sweaty and afraid. Alone in my apartment I hear the unmistakable sounds of someone moving around in the next room. I imagine a strange man bending over my bed—his face obscenely smiling in anticipation of my screams. A shadowy figure in a stocking mask waits for me in the hall. Why doesn't Valdi bark? I wrap myself quickly in a bathrobe and turn on all the lights. No one.

But during the day I am calm and unafraid. The perfect New York girl. When I walk down Madison Avenue, men, and other girls like me, eye me in recognition and admiration. I live here. I jog. Twice a day I treat my face with Erno Laszlo's special soaps and lotions. Once a month my legs are waxed by Mrs. Rugged at Elizabeth Arden. My hair is cut by Harry at Kenneth's and twice a year Marianne puts a series of blond streaks in it—wrapping the silky little clumps in tinfoil and painting them with white paste. My father pays these bills without comment. My clothes have names on the labels. At all times I wear a gold chain and a man's Cartier tank watch—both presents from my parents while I was married—and the Elsa Peretti diamond stud earrings that Jason gave me the last Christmas we were together. My apartment is a treasure. Jason's credit rating is good.

But that is not what I am really like. I have a terrible beauty problem. There is this secret painful business going on inside me that irritates the skin and rubs against the surface, sometimes erupting in tiny sores. My heart makes a lot of noise, too. I can't control it. Sometimes in expensive French restaurants, bending gracefully across the linen tables toward the men who pay for me, I hear my heart knock so loudly that I am sure people are looking around at me from other tables, and that the man will be suddenly afraid and the waiters will shun us. Even in Melon's or Clarke's where I go to eat with better friends, I am often terrified that the noise and grunts of my real system will catch me up in the middle of some polite or witty phrase and give me away.

"What on earth is that terrible noise?" my friend will say.

There are times when I wonder if I could stop this horrible tension by leaving here, by letting my eyebrows grow out and my hair get brown again, and wearing flat shoes and living in the woods. Peace in the woods. Who would notice me there? But then I think maybe the noise and the trouble that I carry around with me would scare the animals and the plants. Scurrying away from me in the forest leaves. That would be worse. For the moment, I try to placate my disease with amenities. A wonderful new picture for the apartment, a challis skirt, a glossy pair of leather boots for the oncoming cold. I wander through the stores in the look, leap, plunge, retreat pattern of the shopper bird. Distracting myself.

Sometimes people say that I am driven, and they are right. But thank God no one ever gets to see the driver. He doesn't drive safely. He doesn't stop or start or slow down when I tell him to. When he is at the wheel I am out of control. And he is a man.

chapter 25

Sunday morning. I lie in bed and stare at the rain falling on the other side of the glass. It's nine o'clock and I'm wide awake, but if I could sleep until noon half the day would be gone. Weekends seem an endless time, with the rest of the world at play, the rest of the world on its way to the country. Two whole days before everyone comes back again and it's all right to be alone.

How will I pass the time? Lying there on this rainy Sunday, I decide to give a dinner party. Cooking for Mike Abrams reminded me that I like to cook. Jason taught me a lot. If I give a dinner party next Saturday night, that will take care of next weekend, at least. Immediately I feel better. My mind starts to hum. Lists of guests. Lists of groceries. Lists of possible menus. Annie and David. Sara and Jim. Mike Abrams, to play the host. The Irvings (it wasn't their fault that Colin came to their party with another girl!). Cold roast chicken stuffed with summer vegetables. Salad in the big bowl with mushrooms. Cold avocado soup to start. Apricot tart with heavy cream for dessert.

As it turns out, the party takes care of the whole week. Everyone is delighted. Sara and Annie both call me to confer at length about what to wear. Plans and counterplans. I find a wonderful Koos Van den Akker dress at Nancy & Co., the little store across from the Carlyle. Pieces of flowered cotton lawn sewn together on a bias. I can't afford it, but I buy it anyway. The day before the party I marinate the chicken and shop for liquor, and the whole thing seems to bring me luck, because the next day just before the guests come, when I am racing around with my hair in two curlers, the telephone rings. It's Joel Stansky.

We chat for a minute and I am relieved to find that we are still friends. He has decided to pretend that that night never happened. It's okay with me. "Listen, Salley," he says, "we don't have a job here right now, but I wonder if you would like to try writing a story for us? We're looking for something personal about living alone in New York, and about being single right after a divorce. I thought of you right away. Do you think you could do it?"

Well, I could try.

The party is wonderful. The women all look beautiful in their summer dresses, Mike Abrams is a gallant and efficient host, and everyone stands on the terrace in the summer twilight. Valdi loves parties too. He lies on his back on the floor with his little round feet in the air. The guests feed him scraps. And when everyone has left, glowing with friendliness and having a good time and the Piesporter I served with the chicken, and the dishes are stacked, Mike Abrams leaves too but in the nicest way. No pass. Just a hug and a kiss.

"You'll make it, kiddo," he says.

And then he's gone too and Valdi and I drink the last

glass of wine in a warm contented haze on the sofa. The next day Mike sends some flowers and the day after that he calls early in the morning.

"Wanna go sailing?" he says. "I'm taking a day off."

It's a clear blue day with traces of autumn in the air, and sailing seems like a wonderful idea. The last sail of the season. So I leave Valdi unwalked and stuff my slicker and Topsiders and sailing things into a bag and dash around the corner to buy bread and cheese and wine for our sailing lunch and put everything in the car and head out of the city for the Yacht Club.

What a day! Mike is in a wonderful mood too, and we are sailing with an old friend of his whom I met once when we were all at college, but haven't seen since then.

"You look just the same," he says.

"Better!" I say.

And he agrees. The water looks calm with a little chop when we start out of the Yacht Club harbor toward the open water of the Sound, but before we even get the sails up the wind begins to rise and there are suddenly huge waves. Autumn squall. Water breaks over the bow of the boat. The decks are awash and I'm glad I stowed everything down in the cabin. I take the helm while the two men struggle with the sails, the mainsail flapping wildly in the wind, the boom creaking and pushing against the mast. The boat thumps down hard between each wave and the bow is tossed up again against the water.

"Jesus Christ," says Mike's friend. "I'm glad I didn't bring my kids."

Soon I am both sick and scared. The waves are getting bigger. Land looks a long way off, and I think that even if the boat capsizes at least it will stop the decks from seesawing back and forth with each swell. The horizon expands and contracts in my stomach. Finally, Mike gets the sails up and we cut the motor, but it's no better. We start on a windward tack, thump, thump, over and back over. Through the haze of sweat in my eyes, cold forehead, churning stomach, I see a group of racing sloops, the nearest one about a hundred yards away, with two people in orange slickers hiking out on the windward side. As I watch, they break out their bright striped spinnakers and turn down the wind. Heading for home. Mike gives me three pills to take. I take them, and then I am afraid to throw up because I might throw up the pills. We turn back. I lie in a miserable hot-and-cold daze against the centerboard, the friend is on the cabin steps with his head between his knees, and Mike sails the boat alone. Then, miraculously, we are back and through the breakwater, and the water is suddenly calm and we tie the boat and the sails come down and it's over.

We sit on the now still decks and talk. I feel relaxed and bombed, totally bombed. Those pills. My body is chewing gum, my body is rubber. Mike took the pills, too. "I was afraid if you were sick it would make me sick and I wouldn't be able to sail," he says.

Now we are both zonked. The decks should be cleaned but we don't care. The friend leaves. I lie in the sun. Mike is reading a biography of Felix Frankfurter, and he sits on the cushions at the back of the boat. He props the heavy book against his knees and smiles and dozes. I lean against him and slip in and out of a delicious sleep, disjointed blue-sky dreams. The water laps at the sides of the boat. The shrouds clank softly against the mast; the sun comes through the rigging. The sounds of the boatyard. Drifting in and out of sleep. The long afternoon.

At twilight, after the sun has set on the other side of the river and it begins to get chilly I get up to leave. Mike wants me to stay. "Now is the time to go when it's still so beautiful," I say. He understands, and we walk out across the docks together. Arms entwined, feet crunching softly on the Yacht Club gravel.

Summer is over.

chapter 26

I can remember now that the first time I saw Josie Davis was in a photograph in the front pages of *Time* Magazine, where she was working as a researcher. *Time* had done a story on hot pants, the latest fashion then, in their "Modern Living" section and researcher Johanna Davis, the copy said, had taken a pair home to model them for her husband and children. There was a leader for the story in the space above the editor's letter and a lighthearted photo of Josie, hamming it up in short pants.

And the first time I heard about her was from my friend Bud Stillman.

"You know, you remind me a lot of a friend of ours named Josie Davis," he said to me one day, and it was the beginning of a kind of friendly joke. Of course, I had never met Josie Davis, but a witticism or a facial expression of mine would recall her and the Stillmans would tell me about it. They compared our lives as well. I heard that Josie, too,

was the daughter of a distinguished man, Herman Manckiewicz, and that she was married to a gentle Ivy-League type
in his forties, Peter Davis. Peter had just finished making an
anti-war documentary for television, *The Selling of the Pen-
tagon*, and everybody was talking about him—especially the
Stillmans. He and Josie had two children. Josie was writing
a novel.

"She's funny just like you, dear," Bud said to me once,
"and she's a little fat like you, too." This made me very
wary.

There were a lot of places where I might have run into
Josie, it turned out, but I only met her once—a meeting en-
gineered by the Stillmans at a dinner party for local liberals
that they gave at their house in Litchfield before a showing
of Peter's documentary. I liked her right away. For one
thing, she was beautiful and not at all fat, with an open
smart face and thick long blond hair. We didn't fall into
each other's arms though. I guess no one really likes to be
told that she looks like someone else.

I remember her in the auditorium after the film, buckling
her rose-colored raincoat around her waist, her hair falling
straight on her shoulders. It was during the McGovern campaign and our hopes were high. She was talking to someone
in the aisle in front of me and when he mentioned that he
was working for McGovern in Washington I heard her say
quietly, "Oh, perhaps you know my brother."

Because Frank Manckiewicz was running McGovern's
campaign and it even looked as if he might win and
straighten out the whole world and everyone was talking
about Frank, too.

And the morning after the party Peter Davis came over to
the Stillmans', because Jason and I were there for the weekend, and we talked and he said how much they wanted to

be friends with us. Morning sun slanting down on the heavy wooden kitchen table. Flowers. Copper pots.

Josie went up to Litchfield to stay with the Stillmans for a while when she had trouble finishing her novel and Bud told me that she wanted to use a title he had found for her, *Crazy Salad*, from William Yeats' poem "A Prayer for My Daughter":

> *It's certain that fine women eat*
> *a crazy salad with their meat.*

But instead, she called the book *Lifesigns*. I read it in paperback sitting beside the swimming pool that summer. Interested although our friendship had never come true. It was a short book and it tried to tell how it was to be an intelligent woman then, but a woman who wasn't angry about being intelligent. There's a whole generation of women like Josie, I sometimes think, not feminists exactly, but feminists in a way. Women who want to stay inside that golden circle society describes, who want to love men, and have pretty dresses and learn to cook and bear children in peace, but who can't help being a little different. And that makes them want to change things.

But about a year after the book came out, Josie was walking with her sons down Charles Street in Greenwich Village and a taxicab accidentally jumped the curb after a collision with another car and hit Josie, throwing her against a mailbox. She was killed instantly.

Somehow though, she's still around for the rest of us. And when Nora Ephron published her first collection of short pieces, she called it *Crazy Salad* and used the Yeats poem as an epigraph. "I would also like to have thanked Josie Davis," she wrote.

And in Jill Robinson's novel *Perdido*, which is about her childhood in Hollywood, there is this female character who lights up the whole narrative. Sharp and funny and beautiful and complicated. Valentine Benedict. In the novel her father is a blacklisted screenwriter; and at the end she is killed in a car crash, thrown out of her little convertible and killed.

And in John Leonard's review of *Perdido* in the *New York Times*, he remembered that Jill and Johanna Davis grew up together, Jill was Dore Schary's daughter and Josie was Mank's daughter and he pointed out that Val Benedict is also Josie Davis.

I don't want to be corny about this, but I did want you to know.

chapter 27

I do the best writing at night, after avoiding the typewriter all day, when there are no more possible excuses, no shopping or vacuuming or telephone calls or walking Valdi. I sit down then, under the desk lamp at the creaky old wooden table I bought for five dollars at the Irvington Thrift Shop and work away. It's been a long time since I wrote at all and it takes me a while to get phrases right. This is the first time I have ever written about my own experience—a far cry from the Laramie police blotter—but I find that almost instinctively I know what do do. For one thing, all day while I am avoiding it I think about it. It's not easy, but I know just how it should sound. Intimate, but not sappy.

My days are still the same old empty days—Central Park, the supermarket, the library—but the work absorbs a lot of energy and a lot of my floundering around. Joel has been terrific. He calls a lot and we had a drink in the Cedar Bar about a block from his office to talk it over. Not as if that night had never happened, but as if we could both afford to skip it. No funny stuff. No this-is-the-only-place-that-serves-Harp-Irish-beer and no coke-in-fancy-snuffboxes and no I'll-probably-fall-in-love-with-you. None of that. He talks about the story and he has a way of making me feel that he knows I will do well, and he discusses it as if it was really going to happen.

And it did, too, I finally finished it, Joel loved it—he called to say so—and they published it in the middle of the August issue, not only quite near the front, but with a big leader for it on that cheesy newsprint-blue-and-white cover they have. *Being Single* by Salley Gardens. Wow. And a lot of people have called to say how much they liked it or how much it meant to them. Abrams and Ed Miller wrote notes and Annie and Sara took me out for a celebratory lunch at La Goulue.

In a way, the most important reaction I got was from my father.

When Jason and I split up, my parents were pretty displeased and I think they blamed the whole thing on me. They didn't say anything, but there was a lot of silence and no reassurance. It would have been nice. And I found out from Jason that they had called him and written to him to make sure that he was all right. But not me. So I stayed away from them after that.

"Dear Salley," my father wrote. "Your mother and I both read and enjoyed your article in the *Village Voice*. I think I am now commencing to grasp an understanding of how you felt at the end of your marriage. I see that you could prefer a career as a newspaper writer to being, as you would call it, just a housewife."

Graceful prose was never my father's strong suit.

So in the wake of all this success, bolstered by my tinny

new confidence, I decided to go out to San Francisco to see Max. The *Voice* even paid me, after all. Strong Salley. Taking-the-bull-by-the-horns Salley. I can't even tell if he wants me to come.

"But I'm so busy now," he said, "but please, please come."

United Airlines Flight 556 leaves Kennedy airport at noon and arrives at San Francisco at two forty-five in the afternoon. The Midwest is green and flat; in the Sierras the mountains are still covered with snow. As we dip down toward the airport I can see the Hayward Bridge and the Bay and the white buildings of the city sparkling in the sun.

Max is late to pick me up at the airport, of course. I search with chagrin among the faces crowded at the gate to meet the incoming flight. I knew he wouldn't be there. Should I go into the Tahiti Bar and have a Mai Tai? For the first time my courage ebbs. I begin to wonder if taking the bull by the horns is such a great strategy. I hate waiting in airports at the end of a trip.

Then, suddenly, Max is there, pushing through the crowds toward me.

"Come on, let's get out of here," he says. He grabs my bag and gives me a big hug and loops an arm around me and everything is all right again. We're off.

I am staying at Max's studio, and when we get there I can see that he has been living somewhere else. The room is coated with plaster dust and most of Max's work has already been removed for the show. One lonely piece, looking like a fat stork, squats in the middle of the room. The bed has been stripped and covered with a red Indian cotton spread, and a white telephone sits on the floor. I had dreamed, at thirty-two thousand feet over Ohio, and over Indiana, and over Nevada, of Max's and my falling into each other's arms on this bed and not getting up for a week. Instead, he looks around the room with distaste.

"Let's go get a drink, for God's sake," he says.

We walk down Kearney Street to Paddy's Irish Bar, a long narrow room with wood paneling and booths where Max spends almost every evening when he is in San Francisco, he says. Everyone says hello. Paddy shakes hands with me. We sit at the bar with Annabelle and Jed, two friends of Max whom I have also met in New York.

I like Annabelle, and I lean over to kiss her on the cheek.

"Hey, hey, Salley's here," says Jed, who is already a little drunk. "When's the big day? When are you two getting married?"

"Maybe sometime in the next twenty years," I say.

No one laughs. I order straight vodka and it takes hold pretty quickly—it's about ten o'clock at night New York time —and by the time I am facing Max at dinner at the Slung Low in Chinatown everything seems a little bit blurry.

"I take it you don't want to get married, Salley," he says. Sarcasm.

"Do we have to talk about it when I'm so sleepy?"

And so most of our first night together is spent in an angry haze. We go back to the studio and I make the bed as Max slams around in the kitchen trying to coax ice cubes out of the refrigerator. Then at last we are in bed and we are as hungry for each other as ever, our anger melts and adds to our passion and we make love and make up and fall asleep together. Sudden and deep.

And in the morning, things are a little better. Max has decided to be nice.

"I've decided to be nice," he says.

He brings me coffee and tells me how glad he is that I have come. He has to go to work, but he doesn't seem to want to and, lying there next to him before he leaves, everything seems in place again. Next to Max is where Salley belongs, I tell him. And we make love again with him lying back and smiling up at me because he wants me and he knows he's going to get me and we come together and the morning light floods in through the windows and outside cars go up and down on Kearney Street.

I have arranged to have lunch with Annabelle at a restaurant called MacArthur Park. We sit in a large room with brick walls on plump cushions on the floor and eat alfalfa sprouts and apples. Glass plates, white wine in carafes, at one corner of the room a dozen birds chirp in an elaborate natural habitat. For a while we chat about the art world; Annabelle works at a small gallery on Sutter Street and she has known Max since he moved to California. Then we talk about men and she tells me how Jed left her to go off with someone else about six months ago and how, after a horrible few weeks when she could tell he had stopped loving her but he hadn't told her he was in love with someone else yet, she had found another lover too. When that happened Jed left the girl he had gone with and came back and hung around her like a puppy dog. "It made him seem so weak," she says, "I'm not sure how I feel about him anymore."

No wonder Jed is drinking too much. But, as we sip our iced Capuccinos and stir them with cinnamon sticks, Annabelle gives me a little appraising look that warns me that she is about to come to the point. Why does there always have to be a point?

"I'm really glad you came, Salley," she says, shifting into low gear. "It's very important for Max that you're here even though he probably doesn't act that way all the time. I hope you're planning to stay awhile."

She stops and gives me a serious serious look. So I take her seriously too and try to explain why I can't stay for long. I live in New York. I am writing another story for the *Voice*.

There is nothing for me to do in San Francisco but be Max's girl. He is very busy. I love Max, but I just got over a very bad time at the end of a marriage and I'm not ready to get married again right away.

"Well, I'm worried about him," Annabelle says, swirling the coffee, which makes creamy brown rings in her glass cup. "He's very impatient and he wants to get married again and have children. It's you he's in love with, but he's not the type of man to wait around."

I wonder if this is a threat.

"What about Amanda?" I say.

"He doesn't care about her," says Annabelle, staring into her glass. "She's a convenience. When she calls at the museum he won't even talk to her. But he knows she will do whatever he wants. She'll wait forever. She wants to be Mrs. Max Angelo and she's convinced that she can make him happy."

"Well, I don't," I say, "I don't want to be Mrs. Max anybody."

We laugh, but Annabelle still looks worried and earnest and I try to change her mood.

"I love Max," I tell her, "and he loves me. We'll work it out, we'll be okay, don't worry."

But as the days go by Max and I seem less and less okay. During the day he is working at the museum and by the time I see him at Paddy's at about seven I am lonely and bored and desperate for loving and he is worn out and surrounded by other people. One night I get to Paddy's first and when Max comes in I see Paddy hand him a gray vellum envelope.

"Amanda left this for you," Paddy says.

I fume. We have a couple of drinks and I am drinking straight vodka again and it doesn't mix well with good intentions. There are a lot of people around us. I talk to one, then another, but what I am really trying to do is figure out how to keep myself from asking Max what is in Amanda's note. You'll only hurt yourself, I warn myself, you'll just make yourself unhappy.

But I lose.

We leave Paddy's and walk down the street back to the little studio, spruced up by me in the long afternoons with fresh flowers and a few books and a new bottle of Chivas and real glasses. I walk silently beside Max.

"Well," I say in this horribly bitchy voice. "And what does Amanda have to say?"

Max gives me a long-suffering look and hands me the note.

It is written on elegant paper in a schoolgirl's handwriting, rounded script.

"I'll always remember those times in Italy this summer," it says. "No matter what you do. I'll always love you."

"I guess she knows you are here," Max says.

I am furious and hurt. So she was in Florence with him then! I was in New York and in trouble and Max didn't have time to come and see me and they were far away in the Tuscan hills together. Sitting on the flagstones in Fiesole and watching the sun set behind the Duomo. Laughing over white wine on sunny terraces. Making love in the long afternoons with the light coming in through wooden shutters. I feel sick.

"What's the matter, Sal?"

"You know perfectly well what's the matter."

"I don't understand you," Max complains. "We've both seen other people, for Christ's sake. If you'd marry me we wouldn't have to. It's you I love. It's you I want to marry. Amanda would give anything to marry me, but I want you."

Somehow, Max's genius for making everything all right doesn't work. We eat a silent dinner at Enrico's, greeting the people we see there with false smiles and lapsing into angry silence with each other. Vodka moods. Afterward we drive back to the studio in the car, it is late and we are drunk. Max drops me off and drives away down Kearney Street to park the car. I go upstairs and take off my clothes and get into bed. Maybe when we are in bed together we will thaw out, I think. But Max doesn't come. I can't sleep. An hour passes. I get up and look out the window. Down at the other end of Kearney Street I can see a parked car that looks like Max's car but I can't be sure. I get dressed and go out. It's about two in the morning and the street is empty as I walk toward the car and as I get close to it I can see that Max has passed out and slumped down in the driver's seat behind the wheel. Parked and passed. And my stupid heart goes out to him. He's as confused as I am, I guess. I go over and open the door and he half tumbles into my arms.

"I love you, Salley," he says. "I love you. If I fuck us up I don't know what I'll do."

He says it over and over again and we walk back up the stairs together and into bed at last, head over heels over head. Max and me. Me and Max. Falling toward each other in a warm delicious sleep.

The next morning we are very gentle with each other. Max has to go to work but we decide to meet at lunchtime and take the Tiburon Ferry over to Sam's Bar and spend the afternoon there on the wooden deck next to the boatyard.

"At least we'll have a chance to be alone," Max says.

And it's a lovely afternoon. Yes. We sit on the open deck and drink beer, leaning back in Sam's giant wooden chairs in that sparkling sunny air they have in San Francisco with sails out in the Bay and the city like a pile of white building blocks across the water. We feel tough and glamorous and in love. We belong together. And as we take the ferry back to town in the fading light with the sun setting crimson behind the Golden Gate Bridge a group of racing sloops on our port side turn for their last buoy and one by one break out their bright spinnakers and scud in front of the ferryboat's bows.

"Let's do it right now," Max says, hugging me as we stand at the railing and watch the red and blue sails and the lights of the city coming closer. "Let's just get married tomorrow. I'll skip work and we'll drive to Reno in the morning and we'll get married and then you can start looking for a house for us. Okay? Okay?" And he danced a little jig of entreaty on the deck.

I don't say no. Who could? It's not the time for saying no, half drunk and all in love, standing at the railing of the Tiburon Ferry in the warm San Francisco twilight.

But I don't say yes.

And the next morning Max goes to work as usual.

chapter 28

I go to the San Francisco Cable Car Barn and stand at the top level where the wooden cars with their bright coloring and gingerbread ironwork are being washed and cleaned. In the dark chamber over the white wooden balustrade of the tourists' gallery I can see the oiled steel cables gliding in snaky figure eights around the giant cogwheels and out through the tunnels under the streets. The heart of the city. On the walls there are daguerreotypes of old cable car scenes. A group of nineteenth century women sit primly on the wooden car benches; women weren't allowed to stand on the car steps and hang on to the railings until 1975. A band of Victorian rowdies in their narrow ties and felt hats tilt their cigars roguishly at the camera. In the corner, a small tombstone commemorates three dogs who guarded the cable station and were cruelly poisoned by burglars. At the middle of the room is the original cable car. Sidetracked forever. THIS CAR IS ONE HUNDRED YEARS OLD. IT WILL NOT HOLD PEOPLE, a sign warns visitors.

As I walk up the steep hill from the barn in the sunlight I am seized by a sharp gust of desire. A painful longing for someone or something that almost doubles me over at the curb. But who am I missing? I ask myself, and there is no answer. Not really Max, and not really Jason, and not really anyone. A yearning handful of dust. An unquenchable emptiness.

Because Max is gone all day I have a lot of time to think. I have lunch with old friends and spend long afternoons reading *The Eustace Diamonds* but even Trollope's melodrama can't keep my mind from daydreaming. It's true, although I wouldn't dare tell Max, that I would sort of like to have children too. Maybe as much as he would. And when I think of what a father he would be, generous and funny and open-hearted and quick to love, I sort of want to have Max's children.

At the beginning, I remember though, I sort of wanted Jason's children too. That feeling of a new person growing inside me, a person who would be Jason's and mine. The irresistible tininess of babies and babies' things.

"Please don't do anything rash," my mother said when I tried to explain these feelings to her.

So Jason and I never got around to it. Perhaps I was too sensible. Trying to wait until, as I said to him, we had somewhere to put them. Maybe I just didn't want Jason's children after a while. He was child enough. Who knows. It's a mistake to think that you decide these things.

But it was true, the idea of living with Max in one of the wonderful wood Victorian houses on a hill above the Bay and giving dinner parties in a big kitchen and being Mrs. Max Angelo and even aceing out Amanda appealed to me a lot. It was me he wanted. I too would have overalls tucked into soft leather boots and T-shirts from Italy and gauzy caftans belted with heavy silver. I too would be one of them. I loved Max.

But I thought he would wait for me.

I thought I could have everything, in time.

And so the days of my visit passed.

There were bad days. One afternoon while I was lying on that lumpy bed reading, just as I had gotten to the part where Lizzie Eustace finds out that the diamonds she thought she had stolen are missing from the escritoire where she hid them in the parlor, there was a knock at the studio door and two museum assistants came to take the last sculpture.

It took them a long time to dismantle it and get it out the door and I sat there determinedly trying to read in spite of the banging and the thumping and the clouds of plaster dust. I had nowhere else to go, really.

But just as the two men were finishing up, I hoped, Max came back and saw the whole thing at a glance—he always did—me crouching at the end of the mattress trying angrily to read, and the noise and the no privacy and there being nowhere else to go.

"Hurry it up, you guys," he said, and they suddenly got a lot more efficient and finished the job in about two minutes. Max walked over to the kitchen and got down a glass and poured himself a whiskey and turned to me, still huddled on the bed.

"I'm sorry, Salley," he said.

"It's not your fault."

"Can't you see that I don't want you to live this way?"

"I don't live this way," I said. "I live in New York."

But I hated fighting with him. It tore me apart. I could always feel it coming, a sinking despairing sort of feeling deep in the pit of my stomach. He didn't like it either, I guess, his eyes would look glassy and sad and his whole face drooped. Max was the man for me after all, and I was the girl for him. We both knew that. Loving Max had liberated me, it had taught me to be my best self, it had shown me what I could do. Max had taught me to be Salley. If I couldn't love Max, who was I?

So we concentrated on pleasing each other. There were times when I wanted to talk, when I thought that if we lay there in bed for a while and were very gentle with each other we could straighten the whole thing out. But Max's idea of friendly behavior was usually making love, and he swept me along with him and afterward we both fell into those deep sleeps. So we never did try to negotiate.

We both knew that I couldn't stay at the studio much longer. The morning I said I thought I should go back to New York, Max was nice about it. He didn't sulk when I called to make an airplane reservation. His show at the museum was scheduled to open in two weeks and we made a lot of careful plans. I would come back for the opening party and spend the weekend. Then Max would come back to New York with me; it would be his first free time since May. Then we would see.

But with Max, plans were always closer to dreams than to responsibility. He lived entirely in the present, in what was there at the moment, and in his work. I knew this, and you'll say I should have known better than to do what I did, but I didn't really have a choice.

I couldn't marry him like that, on the quick, with all my doubts and half out of jealousy and half out of ambition. That's how I got into trouble in the first place. Anyway, marriage made a harpy out of me. And I couldn't stay on in that studio with nothing to do but wait for Max to come home in the evening. And I couldn't just move out there that instant, not without marrying Max. And I couldn't marry Max.

So I went back to New York.

Max drove me to the airport.

"Bye, Salley," he said, and he kissed me.

But after I had walked through the security checks and gotten my ticket stamped and put my baggage on the conveyor belt and when I was almost at the boarding gate with the stewardess ushering people onto the plane I couldn't bear it.

So I ran back across the linoleum floor and back through the security checks and across the lobby and caught up with Max just as he was getting into his car. He looked surprised and I threw my arms around him and hugged him as hard as I could.

I was crying. "Max, I love you, I love you, it's going to be all right," I was saying. "You'll come to New York and we'll get married and we'll have little Maxes and I love you."

He held me hard and he couldn't speak and tears were streaming down my face and making a big wet stain on his jacket.

"It's okay, Sal," he said, "it's okay, I'll come."

People were watching us and then just being in Max's arms made me feel a lot stronger and more my-self—I couldn't stay then with my bags checked and my ticket gone, could I?—so with one last look and a kiss and an I'll-see-you-soon I went back across the lobby and through the security checks again and down the hall to Gate Four and got on the plane and stayed there. I had to, don't you see? Well anyway, I thought I had to. Well anyway, I did.

My plane landed in New York at midnight. I had done a

lot of crying on the flight and I felt awful. No one met me. I took a rattling cab back into the steamy city, trying not to cry again. I had left Valdi at Sara's while I was away and the apartment was empty. No mail. No messages. No one. I poured myself the last drink from a bottle of Scotch in the kitchen and went to bed. In my dreams, Max was wearing a velvet cape with a red silk lining and twirling and twirling to some inner waltz.

But in the morning I was awakened by the telephone ringing and it was Mike Abrams saying how glad he was that I was back and that he had kept the boat in the water because there was an important race coming up and he would like me to crew for him and would I like to have dinner. And when I went over to Sara's apartment to pick up my plants and my mail, Valdi practically wriggled out of his skin, he was so happy to see me. Then Sara and I had lunch at Melon's and she, at least, understood perfectly.

"You've just begun to get on your own feet," she said. "You need more time before you let it happen again."

After lunch and a glass of white wine at Sara's, Valdi and I and the plants went back to my apartment—he had to smell in all the corners to make sure that nothing had been disturbed before he settled down under the desk. And nothing had been disturbed. The rooms were clean and there were fresh sheets because Hester had come while I was gone and everything looked wonderful and I lay on my own bed and pulled up my own quilt and finished reading *The Eustace Diamonds,* savoring the quiet and the privacy and the not waiting for anyone and then I took a nap and when I woke up everything seemed to be back in place again.

Valdi under the desk. Sara and Mike. God in his heaven. My typewriter waiting for me to start work on my next article. The apartment with the lights going on in the city beyond my terrace in the fading light.

And Max Angelo and Amanda and Paddy's and the Kearney Street studio and the sinking feeling they gave me in the pit of my stomach seemed about a million miles away. I was home.

chapter 29

I walk through Times Square late in the afternoon, picking my way through traffic and across subway gratings in the crowds of derelicts—seedy toughs wandering down toward the garment district, shopping bag ladies with their greasy faces. Pot-bellied small businessmen hurrying along in their shiny gray suits.

I am on my way to be interviewed at the *New York Times*.

"Mr. Beard would like to see you, Salley. Would Friday afternoon be all right?"

Outside the long gray New York Times Building with its flashing electric clock, next to the falling-down tenements and the broken windows on the other side of Forty-third Street, a group of City Sanitation workers are picketing the *Times*. An editorial opposed their proposed 30 percent wage hike and so they stand there looking tough and aimless and angry and occasionally breaking into a chant of "*Unfair, un-*

fair, *un*fair," and walking down the block and circling back
to display their sandwich board picket signs.

I go up to the city room gray and grim, on the third floor,
where all the noise blends into the murmur of voices on the
telephone and the clack of typewriters. Everyone looks pur-
posefully seedy and colorless, as if to blend into the neighborhood. Or as if to be a good reporter you had to look bad.

("Am I a good looker?" I am standing on a chair in my
parents' bedroom, and I have found my mother's watch,
which has been lost for frantic hours. She inherited it from
her mother; it was under the carpet. I am eight.

"Am I a good looker?"

For a moment there is a strained silence. My parents stare
uncomfortably up at me. What can I mean? Have they
raised a tiny narcissist? Then they realize what I am saying
and they smile to each other and lift me off the chair with a
big hug.

"Yes, Salley, you are very, *very* good at looking.")

"How are you doing, Salley?" Jack Beard asks, glancing
over my new resumé and a copy of the *Village Voice* story.
We sit in his little cubicle at the head of the city room and
through his windows come the chants of the striking Sanitation workers.

"*Un*fair, *un*fair, *un*fair."

I tell him that I am divorced now, and that I am more
eager than ever to go to work.

"I do know of a job that might interest you," he says. "It
pays pretty well. It's an opening on the public relations staff
of the syndicate that runs the Lyons fund."

My heart sinks, my head swims. This conversation is important. You aren't summoned to the *Times* to pass the time
of day. I sense that this is a test, but I am not sure whether
it is a test to see how serious I am about getting a job—in
which case I should say yes, I *am* interested—or if it is a test

to see how serious I am about working as a reporter in general and for the *New York Times* in particular—in which case I should say no.

"Well, I think I would rather wait and try to get a reporting job," I say, hesitating a little.

"Okay, Salley." He sounds relieved, or am I imagining it? "I'll let you know if anything else comes up here."

And I am ushered out through the city room and past the security guards to the elevator.

"Unfair, unfair, unfair."

I am sailing again with Mike and Bob, the friend from college. We have sailed out past City Island and into Long Island Sound and at lunchtime we anchor off Glen Cove to swim in and see if we can buy a hot dog. It's September, but the water is still warm.

Bob grew up in Glen Cove and he wonders if he will see his parents' friends the Tannenbaums on the beach. We dive together off the stern—Mike stays with the boat—and swim away from *Dreamstuff* through the heavy opaque green water to the line of white floats that marks the beach swimming area. As we cross the line, a man in a rowboat veers toward us, cutting across our path.

"Are you from that boat?" he says, waving an oar in Mike's direction. "Then you can't swim here, you haven't paid admission."

We are treading water at the float line and Bob begins an argument with this summertime vigilante about our legal right to land below the tideline. Bob is a lawyer too. And when the man in the rowboat is unconvinced, Bob asks if he knows the Tannenbaums.

"We're looking for the Tannenbaums," he says.

But the man is adamant and we are both getting tired from treading water and so we swim back to the boat and clamber up the rope ladder to the deck. Mike has been watching the whole scene and laughing. He makes a big salad, and there is a fresh loaf of bread that I brought from Dumas, and Normandy butter, and we have lunch on the upper deck and drink rosé wine in the sun.

Once when I was visiting a school friend on Great Inagua, a little island in the British Bahamas, an unpainted rickety sloop with patched and ragged sails hove into the little harbor one afternoon. It was a boatload of Haitian refugees and when they got to about thirty feet offshore they began to jump over the sides of the boat and swim for it. Free at last. But it was against the law. Matthew Town was not a legal Port of Entry. So the town's only law enforcement officer, a plump constable in a starched white uniform with epaulets, went down to the beach on his official motor scooter to tell the ragged refugees that they couldn't land.

They didn't argue about their legal rights to land below the tideline. They didn't ask if the Tannenbaums were there. Instead they just went right on disembarking, some swimming, some rowing leaky little dinghies, tossing their bundles of belongings onto the beach and going back for more. Crying out to each other in a strange language. The women with big loop earrings and their heads wrapped in bright scarves. The men with their trousers rolled up for wading. The water was clear and blue and we stood on the embankment and watched the scene. Summer friends. High wind in Inagua.

Finally Roger Fox, the town doctor, came down to the beach with his old shotgun and fired a few shots into the sloop's rigging and the Haitians beat it back to their boat. A huge crowd had formed, chattering and exclaiming about the danger as the Haitian boat sailed out of sight around the point. Some of the men had gotten ashore and were hiding in the bush. The boat would land farther down the coast and the angry Haitians would come back overland. Ten of the men had been captured and were herded into the town jail. We saw them marched down the street, looks of tired resignation on their creased brown faces. Left, right, left, right. Stella's mother walked over to the jailhouse to read to the new prisoners from the Bible. Her father gave John a pistol and the two armed men sat up all night on the broad verandahs of the house, hidden in the shadows of the breadfruit trees.

In New Hampshire, I used to swim out into the lake toward the mountains. The water was clear, caressing me like cool heavy air. Everything was austere brown and green in that landscape, shingled boathouses, some orange shutters way across the lake. Below me the sun's reflection rippled off the sandy bottom and I saw through the water the huge cement block and chain that secures the raft we put out in the spring. I looked back at our boathouse and saw my family arrayed along the beach in the distance. Valdi anxiously waiting at the foot of the stairs to the deck. My father, sitting on a director's chair in earnest conversation with a friend and colleague who had come over from Dartmouth for the day. Jason, tall and slender at the water's edge looking out at me. When I landed, coming back into shallow water, guiding myself with my hands along the bottom and putting my feet down at the last minute, he said:

"Why did you go out so far?"

Of course, I realize with a start, about three days beforehand, I am going to miss Max's opening. I call him to apologize, to worry, to hope that it's all right, and to ask when he will be coming to New York after it's over.

"Well, don't worry about it, Salley," he says. "Amanda is giving a big dinner party before the opening and I guess she would have been pretty pissed off if I hadn't been there."

I know that this is supposed to goose me into coming. To get me on the next plane. To remind me that Max doesn't need me. To show me that I could lose him.

Instead it makes me angry.

"I'm glad to know that you're so well taken care of," I say.

"Yes," Max agrees, "I am very well taken care of."

Later that night the telephone rings and it's Max, mooning and drunk and sorry. Oh Salley. Oh Max.

"Couldn't you just come right now? Please, oh please. We won't even go to the fucking opening, we'll just go off somewhere and be together, oh please, Salley, come now."

"Why can't you just come here, then?" I say. "We'll stay in my apartment and make love and drink whiskey." But by now we are both crying, long silences, and when we finally hang up with our problems still hanging on I cry for a long time. And Max slumps in a phone booth somewhere, his eyes glassy and sad, his whole face drooping.

Sara and I have lunch or a drink together almost every day now. She and Jim live about a block away from me and she would like to marry him, but he has already had three disastrous marriages. A nymphomaniac, a woman he left after a year, and his only son's mother who is now living in Katmandu with his former best friend. He doesn't want to get married again. It's because he loves Sara that he doesn't want to marry her, he tells her, and because I can sort of agree with him but still be completely on Sara's side I can help her. We talk a lot, and often the three of us have dinner.

So when I go to my post office box in the lobby of my building one morning and there is an odd-looking letter from Max, a letter I wasn't expecting, I head out of the building and down the block toward Sara's before I even open it. I slit the top of the envelope and unfold the paper. I'm standing on the corner of Eighty-second Street and Lexington

Avenue, across from Lascoff's drugstore, and a taxicab and a red Plymouth are stopped at the light when I read the letter. One moment in time.

"I love you," it says in Max's black-ink scrawl. "But I am going to marry Amanda."

That's all. I go up to Sara's apartment knowing that there's no appeal for me and Max now, and crying, and I know he means it and that he has already told Amanda and that he told her because she would make it happen, and it's what he wants, to get married, and I blubber all this out in Sara's armchair.

She gives me a Valium and a cup of tea and I sit there stunned. Looking out at the street. I knew it; I knew it! In a way, though, I feel relieved. Now I can really start from scratch, I tell myself. I'm not even lonely. I'm working and I have friends and a life of my own. Then I burst into more tears. If I had to do it again, I know the same thing would happen. But I wish it hadn't. I really wish it hadn't.

"I wonder if you would like to come in for another interview," Red Beaumont says. "We may have an opening for a writer in the religion department."

So on Thursday afternoon I put on my gray flannel slacks and my black velvet blazer, because it's getting colder now, and I trek down to the *Newsweek* offices on Madison Avenue. I like the art deco brass doors on the elevators. It seems a year since I have been here, and this time I go right to Red Beaumont's office and we talk like old friends. He tells me how much he liked my article in the *Voice* and I tell him the next one will be even better.

"You should be aiming higher than the *Voice*," he says.

At the end of the conversation he asks if I am free for a minute to meet Dan Arman. He knows perfectly well I am free for a minute. Dan Arman is the editor of *Newsweek*.

Beaumont calls downstairs to the executive suite, I suppose, and we go down together in the elevator to another floor with parquet floors and a pretty receptionist and paintings on the walls. Arman's office is in a sunny corner and there is a Persian carpet and on the walls, pictures of Arman with important people.

"Come in, come in," he says. "Sit right down."

I sink into a white armchair and I like him right away with his serious face and his reading glasses and his earnest good looks. We talk about magazines and writing. I am relaxed and funny. I tell him the story of my career. The top guy never reads a resumé, I find out later; you tell him your background in person. He says he liked my piece in the *Voice*. I tell him the next one will be even better.

"You should be aiming higher than the *Voice*," he says.

So I went to work as a writer at *Newsweek*. At first I was in the religion section as a try-out writer and later I became an editor of the section they call "Lifestyle." Fashions and feathers. I wrote cover stories. I won promotions. I made money. And that other part of my life, my being a wife and not having a job and looking for one, and then my being single and learning about men and finding out the hard way that even love doesn't make things work—that part of my life was over.

I went to see Jason last summer in Cambridge, Massachusetts, where he lives now.

"I've changed," he said. "The year after we split up I changed. I didn't have much money, and I stopped eating meat. So I lost weight and I was alone a lot and I thought about the things you said. I've changed."

It seemed he was right, and it was a wonderful day. A day of the first water. We walked around the Harvard campus in a light rain and talked gently about the difficulties of loving.

We should know. But there is no going back and unraveling those old mistakes, although there are plenty of times now when I don't think I'll ever get married, or have children, or love anyone again in the wonderful simple he'll-take-care-of-me way that I loved Jason once. Or ever love again at all, really. I'm not very tough, if you must know, but that's a secret.